"So, want me to pick you up for the singles meeting this week?" Tate asked.

Faith looked at him, then away. "I'm not sure. I think some people are pairing us up."

Tate reached out and took her free hand in his, liking the touch of her skin, the warm softness. "Hey, let people talk. We know we're friends."

"We *are* friends. I cherish that." She looked away again, then took a deep breath. "But what if I fall for you?"

Tate watched her as she stared at the water. "Why not see where being together leads us?" He raised her hand and kissed the back of her fingers.

She gazed into his eyes and Tate saw the confusion in hers. Then she smiled. "Okay, but no romance for a while. Let's just see what happens as friends."

"No romance." The minute he said the words, he wanted to take them back. He wanted to bring her flowers and watch her smile.

He'd honor the promise. "For now," he added.

Books by Barbara McMahon

Love Inspired

The Family Next Door
Rocky Point Reunion
Rocky Point Promise

BARBARA McMAHON

was born and raised in the southern U.S., but settled in California after spending a year flying around the world for an international airline. She settled down to raise a family and work for a computer firm, and began writing when her children started school. Now, feeling fortunate to be able to realize a long-held dream of quitting her day job and writing full-time, she and her husband have moved to the Sierra Nevada of California, where she finds her desire to write is stronger than ever. With the beauty of the mountains visible from her windows, and the pace of life slower than that of the hectic San Francisco Bay Area, where they previously resided, she finds more time than ever to think up stories and characters and share them with others through writing. Barbara loves to hear from readers. You can reach her at P.O. Box 977, Pioneer, CA 95666-0977. Readers can also contact Barbara at her website, www.barbaramcmahon.com.

Rocky Point Promise
Barbara McMahon

Love Inspired

Recycling programs
for this product may
not exist in your area.

LOVE INSPIRED BOOKS

ISBN-13: 978-0-373-87724-9

ROCKY POINT PROMISE

www.LoveInspiredBooks.com

Printed in U.S.A.

For it is by grace you have been saved, through faith—and this not from yourselves, it is the gift of God.

—*Ephesians* 2:8

To Nanci and Judy, knowing you both has enriched my life. Here's to another year of SKC!

Chapter One

Three men burst into the clinic's reception area. One carried a wet, hysterical child. Another dripped water and blood from a gash on his forehead. The last one supported the dripping man.

Marjorie O'Brien yelled for the doctor and nurse from her receptionist's desk. For an instant there was total bedlam. The child screamed. The men called for the doctor. Marjorie ran around the reception desk to help as much as she could. Behind them more people pressed into the small waiting area.

Faith Stewart heard the commotion and ran into the crowded waiting room. A highly skilled triage nurse with several years' experience in a big city emergency room and trauma center, she knew an emergency when she heard one. A quick triage assessment of each showed her the bleeding man in the sheriff's uniform needed more immediate help than the crying child.

The mother tried frantically to calm the child, who was probably more scared at the turmoil surrounding him than anything else. For an instant, Faith felt she was back at the county hospital in Portland rather than the normally quiet clinic in Rocky Point, Maine.

"The doc needs to see to them right away," the man holding the child shouted. "As you can see…"

Dr. Mallory rushed in, assessing the situation in an instant.

"Faith, help Sheriff Johnson into the first exam room and take care of him. Marjorie, get the child's family into room two." The doctor then turned to the others. "If the rest of you'd wait outside, I think it'll help us get things sorted out and under control here."

In seconds, the wailing child was carried to room two while Faith went to assist the sheriff. The gash on his head continued to bleed, and the water from his clothes puddled at his feet. He leaned heavily on the man next to him.

"I'll get you wet," he said, his words slurring slightly as she reached to shore him up on the side opposite the other man.

"I won't dissolve," she said, pulling his arm over her shoulder. With the other man helping, she managed to get all six-feet-plus of Tate Johnson to the exam room and on the examining table. He leaned back, closed his eyes and gave a soft moan.

"What happened?" she asked as she swiftly began a more extensive exam to see if there were any other critical injuries. Not seeing any, she began to address the gash on his forehead.

"The little boy fell into the sea at the marina," the other man said. "Tate dove in to rescue him."

Tate kept his eyes closed as Faith began to clean the gash, gently pushing his thick dark hair out of the way. She noted that the cut would need stitches. At least that was the only injury she could see. Had the blow been hard enough to cause a concussion?

"Fastest thing I ever saw. In less than a second after the kid fell in, Tate raced down the dock, shucked his utility belt and dove into the water. Don't know what would've happened if he hadn't been walking by the marina park. The mother was frantic, the father didn't even see the child fall in. Kid's too little to swim."

A soft groan sounded again when she pressed a bit too hard.

"Sorry. I need to clean this so it doesn't get infected," she murmured, trying to be gentle, knowing, no matter what, it had to hurt.

"Salt water probably killed any germs," Tate said, his eyes still closed.

She glanced at the other man. "So how did he get this gash?"

"One of the fishing boats coming in too fast. Old Jesse's been warned about it before. Anyway, he didn't see them in the water. Tate had the kid by then, but before anyone could alert the skipper, Jesse rammed his boat right into the two of them." He gestured animatedly as he spoke. "Tate turned at the last minute to shelter the child. Lucky he wasn't knocked unconscious or they both might have drowned."

Faith knew by the excited way the man related the incident that he would be retelling it again and again. She worked swiftly and competently, admiring the way the sheriff had reacted so quickly to help someone in need.

"Is the kid okay?" Tate asked.

"Dr. Mallory's with him now," Faith said. "From my brief assessment when you came in, I'd say he's terrified and soaking wet, but he'll be fine. I think he's scared more than anything. And if you sheltered him from the boat, probably the dunking in the sea was the worst of it." The cut was a bit jagged, she hoped it wouldn't scar.

Faith quietly continued her ministrations. She'd seen much worse in her days in the E.R. Though, for the man lying so quietly, it probably hurt like crazy.

She hadn't met Sheriff Johnson before, though she'd been in town for five weeks. From what others had mentioned in passing, he appeared to be well-liked. This certainly wasn't the way she would have picked to be introduced.

"So, how's our hero?" the doctor asked, coming in a moment later. "John, thanks for getting him here," he said to the other man.

"No problem. Can't have the sheriff bleeding at the docks—gives the town a bad image."

All three men laughed, though Tate's ended in a moan as he opened his eyes and tried to focus.

John touched him on the shoulder. "I'm taking off, man. Call if you need a ride home."

"Thanks," Tate said.

The doctor assessed the wound and confirmed Faith's prediction that stitches were required.

"And I expect you have a mild concussion," he told Tate as he washed his hands in preparation for closing the wound. "How bad it is, we'll have to wait and see."

"All I know is my head's killing me," Tate said, closing his eyes again.

"It'll probably hurt for a while. I'll get you some pain meds once we assess things," the doctor said as he drew up a stool and prepared to stitch the gash. Faith quickly had a sterile kit at his fingertips, the lidocaine already drawn.

The work was done quickly and efficiently. Faith stood by, helping as needed. Despite herself, she continued to admire the sheriff for his stoic endurance during the uncomfortable procedure.

Once finished, the doctor asked Tate if his folks could pick him up and watch him for any signs of concussion. "Just for a day or two. Until we know for certain you didn't sustain any further damage."

"They took off for Boston a couple of days ago. I'll manage on my own. I don't want to have them cut their vacation short just for this," he said, sitting up. "Whoa." He closed his eyes and almost fell over.

"Yeah, I thought you might be a bit off," the doctor said, catching him and then easing him back onto the table. "Faith, please ask Marjorie to call around for someone to bring him some dry clothes. We'll get him comfortable and keep him here for a while under observation. I don't want him wandering around with that knot on his head until I know for sure he's not more seriously injured." The doctor looked at Tate. "And if it does look like you're worse off than I think, we'll either keep you here overnight or send you to the hospital in Portland."

When Tate didn't argue with the doctor, Faith figured the man was probably in worse shape than he expected. Dynamic men like him usually ignored injuries or tried to minimize them. Common sense wasn't always an obvious attribute when you were injured or ill.

She went back to the reception area, where Marjorie was mopping the floor.

"This is why I told the doctor we needed more

help," the receptionist was saying to the waiting patient. The room was empty now, except for Flo Bradshaw, waiting for her appointment to see the doctor.

"Quite a bit of excitement, I heard," she said when Faith came in.

"Everyone's taken care of now," Faith said with a smile. She liked Mrs. Bradshaw, who was having trouble with arthritis and came in weekly as they tried to adjust her medication to ease the pain.

Marjorie gave her a dirty look and continued mopping up the last of the water from the floor.

"Dr. Mallory asked if you'd call someone to bring dry clothes for the sheriff," Faith said to the receptionist, keeping her voice pleasant. Since she'd started work at the clinic five weeks ago, she had received nothing but thinly veiled hostility from Marjorie.

"I've already had a bunch of calls concerning Tate. Word travels fast in Rocky Point. You don't need to worry any," Marjorie snapped, wringing out the mop. "One of the Kincaid boys'll bring a change of clothes. Zack said Tate could go home with Joe. Tate's folks are out of town for the week." She threw a triumphant look, as if showing Faith how much more she was tapped into the life of the residents of Rocky Point.

Which, of course, she would be, Faith acknowledged. Marjorie had lived here all her life. Faith was the interloper who had been hired for the nurse position that Marjorie's niece had also applied for.

Faith nodded, trying not to let the tension between her and the receptionist get to her. She prayed for patience every day. She hoped one day Marjorie would at least be cordial, even if they never became friends.

Joe Kincaid was her landlord, the owner of the apartment she'd rented when she'd moved to town.

The one-bedroom unit was near the water, over an aerobics studio, and an easy walk to the clinic. She was still in the process of decorating, but already loved living there. It was larger than the small apartment she'd had in Portland and cost less to rent. One of the many advantages of starting over in a new town.

"What happened to the child?" Mrs. Bradshaw asked.

"He was only scared. Doc Mallory took care of him and sent him and his parents on their way. She seemed as scared as her son. I hope they've learned to take better care of the youngster. Kids can get into mischief in a heartbeat. How's Tate?" Marjorie asked, before Faith could speak. She swiped the mop one last time and dumped it into the bucket at her feet.

"Fine." Faith would not talk about a patient in the public waiting room. She held the door to the hallway for Marjorie, and the receptionist stomped past her and pushed the bucket back down the hall to the utility room where she could empty it.

"I'll go check on him myself when I dump this," she muttered as she went past.

Faith followed her into the hall and, once the door to the reception area closed, replied, "I don't think we should discuss our patients where other patients can hear."

"Now you look here, missy. Flo Bradshaw's known Tate since he was in diapers. She's just as concerned as the rest of us."

Faith nodded, refusing to reveal anything. If the doctor saw fit to keep Marjorie informed, that was his prerogative. She was not going to violate patient confidentiality.

Please, Lord, help me maintain my cool. Sometimes

*I feel like Paul. He had a thorn in his side and I think
You've sent Marjorie to be the thorn in mine. She does
good work, Lord. Help me to always see that and not
get upset by her snippy ways.*

Faith went to the small alcove that held one of the
office computers and updated the file on Tate Johnson.
She had faith that somehow the Lord was working all
this to the good. She was still new in her faith, having
been brought to the Lord when a life-threatening disease had knocked her for a loop. None of the foster
parents she'd lived with had taught her much about
faith and the Lord. Anything she knew, she'd discovered after the nurse on the oncology ward had sat
down with her, brought her a Bible and shared the
good news. She'd been astonished the God of the universe had time to deal with her puny problems. But
she'd felt His presence more than once over the past
two years and knew it was true. Not that life was perfect or even easier. But somehow, knowing she wasn't
alone made it more than bearable—it made life a joy.

Diagnosed with ovarian cancer, she'd had an uphill
battle physically and psychologically. The illness had
radically changed her life and altered all her previous
goals. It had also ended her career as an E.R. nurse at
the hospital—at least until she recovered her prechemo
energy.

And ended the relationship she'd had with a man
she loved.

Alone in the world, she had to make a living and
found that the slower pace of life and the relatively
calm clinic work suited her perfectly. "Thank You
again, Father, for letting me find this job," she murmured as she hit the Save key on the computer.

When Joe Kincaid showed up with a change of

clothes twenty minutes later, Faith showed him to exam room one. She checked back a few minutes later. Tate had changed, with Joe's help, and was lying on a freshly covered examining table. Once the doctor released him, Joe'd be back to pick him up. The sheriff's eyes were closed when Faith stepped in, but he slitted them a little to look at her.

"Hi, Faith. Heard you're holding on to this one for a while," Joe said with a grin.

"Just till we know if the blow caused more injury than we can see," she said with a friendly greeting to Joe.

"He's got a hard head…how's the boat, is what I want to know." Joe winked. "You'll let me know when he's ready to go?" When Faith nodded, he touched Tate on the shoulder and headed out. "I'll give Marjorie my cell number and she'll find me."

When Joe left, Tate rolled his head gingerly and looked at her. "We haven't been formally introduced. I'm Tate Johnson."

"Faith Stewart. I'm glad to meet you, but not under these circumstances." She pulled the stool near and looked at him, touching his forehead, testing for fever. He felt cool to the touch.

"I should've stopped by earlier. Joe told me he rented the apartment. How do you like Rocky Point?" he asked.

"I like it a lot. Close your eyes. You can still talk and I know the light's bothering you," she said, pushing the lamp away and pulling down the shade to keep the light off his face.

"Doc said the boy was okay." He closed his eyes.

"I didn't see him before he left, but I heard he was mostly scared. You saved him."

"The Lord put me in the right spot at the right time. There were enough people on the dock to help me out when we got within range. The tide's going out, so it could have been a lot worse."

"Umm. It would have been easier without the boat that rammed into you." She liked that he gave credit to the Lord. Another Christian. And one comfortable talking about the Lord. She still felt shy about that sometimes.

"There is that," he concurred.

Faith studied him for a moment. Thick, dark lashes brushed his cheeks. His brows were nicely shaped. The dark hair and tanned skin contrasted with the white bandage now covering the stitches. His face was a little thin, not quite gaunt. When standing he was at least six feet tall. And well built. She hadn't felt an ounce of fat when helping him into the exam room. In top physical shape, and gorgeous to boot, he looked out of place lying on the examining table. He was clearly a man of action.

She glanced at his left hand. Not wearing a ring. She sighed. Not that it should matter to her. She'd moved here to start a new life and that did not include getting involved with anyone for quite a while. The pain of Allen's betrayal had shaken her hope for a normal family life. She was working on forgiveness. His timing had been lousy, but she could understand his fear and flight. Understanding didn't make it easier, but at least she knew the reason he'd let her down.

The sheriff's dark hair was drying every which way. The few times she'd seen him around town, he'd worn a hat. Had he lost it when he dove into the water? Joe Kincaid had brought jeans and a T-shirt and socks.

Tate's shoes were near the wall, obviously still wet. His feet dangled over the edge of the examining table, emphasizing his height. His eyes remained closed, but she knew they were a warm chocolate-brown. She watched as he breathed slowly and steadily. His shoulders were broad and his chest muscular, nicely defined by the soft cotton T-shirt. She expected his size gave the people in town a feeling of safety. She'd feel safe around such a man.

She'd also felt a frisson of awareness. In looks, he had it all. Was he also a good man—one a person could depend on?

"How's the pain?" she asked softly.

"Manageable. Doc gave me something. I'm glad the little boy's okay."

"You're a hero," she murmured, echoing what others had said.

"Naw, just where the Lord had me." He opened one eye and looked at her. "What brought you to Rocky Point? We don't get too many single people moving in. Most seem to leave for the big city. Family here?"

"No family. I wanted a change from Portland. A new start. The town really appealed to me."

"How so?"

"Well, when I was a kid, one of my families brought me here for vacation. I loved it. So when I was looking to relocate away from the city, I thought about Rocky Point first. And as an extra blessing, they needed a new nurse here at the clinic." She sighed with contentment. "So I got the job, found a perfect apartment the same day…and here I am."

He closed his eye and smiled. "A God thing," he murmured.

"I beg your pardon?"

"When things like that fall into place without much effort on our part, I figure it's a God thing. He's directing your path and sweeps away any impediments."

"A God thing," she repeated. She had never thought about it in those terms. Mostly, she considered herself lucky. But if the Lord was directing her life now, it made sense. He'd sweep away any barriers in placing her exactly where He wanted her.

"How many families do you have?" he asked a moment later.

"What?"

"You said one of your families brought you here for vacation, how many do you have?"

"Oh, they were foster parents," she explained. "I had three. My mom died when I was about four, my dad before that. No other relatives."

She'd been on her own since she'd turned eighteen. As a lonely child she'd excelled in school, which enabled her to go on to college through all the scholarships she'd qualified for. She was used to not having family. She'd really missed the support a family would offer when she'd been sick. Her last foster parents had visited her in the hospital, but they hadn't seen each other in a while, so the visit was more awkward than comforting. Visits from her colleagues had been more supportive, though she appreciated the efforts of her foster family.

"Three families? Still in contact with them?"

"With the last one. Even after I aged out of the system, they let me come to their home during college breaks. It's been a few years now since we've had much contact. I didn't stay in touch with the other two. The first family moved out of state when I was ten. I was only in the second one for a year, and not a happy time." No matter what, foster care could never replace a real family.

"No other relatives?" he mumbled.

She shook her head. "No—none the state of Maine could locate." She'd been too young to remember her own parents much, just some hazy memories and a couple of pictures that had traveled with her.

"So you'll probably want a huge family with a dozen kids," he murmured.

Like that would ever happen, she thought sadly. Once upon a time she had hoped for just such a future, but after her hysterectomy, she knew that was not going to happen. She hoped the Lord had something wonderful in store for her. But, all things considered, she was grateful to have found a niche in Rocky Point. And to be alive.

The silence allowed the soft hum of the fluorescent lights to be heard. Dr. Mallory had asked her to watch Tate for any signs that the slight concussion was worsening. The clinic was quiet now that the emergency was past. The doctor and Marjorie could handle the patients who had appointments—he wanted her with Tate. She sat patiently, watching, waiting. She offered a prayer for his speedy recovery and thanks for his rescue of the little boy.

Tate opened his eyes slightly to see if Faith was still in the room. She was so quiet he couldn't hear her. She smiled gently and he closed his eyes, fighting the pounding pain. The medicine had taken the edge off, but his head throbbed steadily in rhythm with his heartbeat.

Lord, thank You for letting me be there when the little boy fell into the water. And for the help of those

who were nearby. Bless that child and his parents. And
please send me wherever there's a need that I can help
with. And if You could ease this headache, I'd really
appreciate it.

He dozed a little, waking when he moved his head
and the pounding spiked.

"Are you comfortable?" Faith asked.

He liked her voice. It was low and soft; feminine
and sweet. And it suited her. Her hair was blond, short
and curly, framing her pretty complexion. Her blue
eyes were the color of a morning sky in spring. The
smile she gave him seemed to light up her face.

"I'm okay. Or will be, I'm sure." He hated being
flat on his back. He was rarely sick and knew he was
a typical male—he didn't like being out of commis-
sion. How long was this headache going to last? If it
would just diminish a bit, he'd be on his way. Right
now it was like drums playing in his brain.

"You took a nasty hit to the head. It'll take a while
to recuperate." She placed her hand on his forehead
again.

He felt the cool touch. What a caring profession—
nursing. He'd only just met the new nurse in town, but
guessed she was a good one. At least from his immediate experience she was.

"Your parents are in Boston I heard you say?" she
asked a minute later.

"For a vacation. First one they've taken in a few
years. They'll be home before the wedding."

"Yours?" she asked.

He grinned and shook his head, wishing a second
later he'd merely told her no.

"Joe and Gillian's. They're getting married the

weekend after Labor Day. I'm in the wedding party. Will I be going with a big bandage?"

"Probably not. The stitches come out in ten days. You'll have a rakish scar, which won't fade by the wedding. But think of it as adding to your mystique."

He heard the teasing note in her voice and smiled. He could get to like this Rocky Point newcomer.

"No mystique when you're a homegrown boy. Born and raised here," he said.

"Loved it and never left?" she asked.

"Love it, but couldn't wait to leave when I was eighteen. I went to college, got on the Boston P.D. My dad had a stroke a few years ago. I came home to help out and, like you—a job was there for the taking." No need to tell her how much he'd wanted to leave Boston by that time. Wherever he went, he ran into memories of Mandy. He and his wife had only been married a year when she was diagnosed with breast cancer. After a hard-fought eleven months, she died. He didn't know if he'd ever get over her death, try as he might with prayer, community involvement and family.

"Another God thing?" she asked.

He was quiet a moment. Was it a God thing He took her home so soon? She'd only been twenty-five years old.

"I'm not sure I'd call it that," he said slowly, the pain of his loss still an ache in his heart. He knew he'd always miss her. Nothing had been the same since she died. He did his best but his heart was forever hurting.

"How's your father now?" Faith asked.

"He's doing okay. He made almost a complete recovery. At least he can still work, so that's a blessing. I'd hate for him to be home all day driving my mother nuts."

"Do you miss Boston?" she asked.

"No." That sounded abrupt. "I'm glad to be back in Rocky Point. My parents won't be around forever. Living here, I'm close to them and to friends I've had all my life. There's a lot to be said for a small town. You must think so or you wouldn't have moved here."

"I do think so. I needed a slower pace of life. I felt I'd have an easier time making friends and finding a safe neighborhood to live in that's lovely at the same time. Portland's a bit impersonal." Her eyes lit up. "And I can't beat my new apartment—I've got a view of the sea and I can walk to the marina in two minutes."

Of course, she hadn't expected Marjorie's hostility. But what was life without a bit of conflict? Following the Lord didn't mean it would be easy, just that she would not alone.

"Do you sail?" he asked.

"I've never tried it. Still, I love watching the sailboats and the speedboats from my bedroom window. Maybe one day."

"I'm glad you rented that apartment," Tate said. "It was empty for a while."

"So Joe said when I first saw it. And I didn't realize until I moved in that Gillian and Joe were engaged. She owns the aerobics studio under my apartment. She's been so nice and has been worried about her music bothering me, since I'm usually there when she has classes. The place is totally quiet most evenings, except the two when she's open. But she's finished by eight, which is perfect for me." She smiled. "I've told her it's no big deal, but she's insisting on taking me to lunch to make it up to me."

Tate nodded, frowning a second later.

"How're you feeling? Do you want something to drink or eat?"

"Maybe some water," he said. His throat felt raw. He'd swallowed a gulp or two of seawater when Jesse's boat hit him. He hoped one of his deputies cited the fisherman. Too often he came flying into the marina, with a wake that could damage boats moored there.

Faith was there a second later, lifting his head and shoulders and holding a cup to his lips. He drank it all.

"You *were* thirsty," she said, easing him back down.

"How soon can I leave?"

"Soon as you feel like it, I think. Want to try to sit up again?"

"Yeah. I need to get going. Joe'll want to leave to get home to his daughter, Jenny. If I'm not ready, he either has to stay in town or send Zack back for me."

"Let's see if you can sit, then," she suggested.

He opened his eyes, glad the room had stopped spinning. He looked at the nurse as she leaned closer and put her arm beneath his shoulders. Her soft blond hair shone in the light. Her blue eyes stared at him. Her smile was gentle. She helped him sit up and when she took away her arm, he wished she still held on.

The room stayed where it was supposed to.

"Want to stand?" she asked a minute later. She hadn't moved away, in case he needed her.

He was impressed by her patience. She didn't fidget or try to hurry him along.

"Sure," he said.

Again she put her arm around him and helped him stand. The room held steady.

"I don't advise you to put on your shoes," she said a second later. "They have puddles of water in them."

"Ruined, most likely. Salt water and leather don't

normally mesh." He took a couple of steps with Faith right by his side. Standing beside her, he gauged her height at around five-seven, and she was a bit on the slender side. Almost too thin—a few more pounds wouldn't hurt. Not that he was an expert. Or even interested. All he wanted now was to get home, sleep through the night and be back to normal in the morning.

"It seems as if you're good to go, Sheriff," she said. "I'll let the doctor know. He wants to see you before you leave."

Tate nodded carefully and stood when she left. He walked around the small exam room a couple of times before Dr. Mallory entered. No dizziness, no double vision. The pounding was down to a manageable level.

"Ready to leave?" the doctor asked, studying Tate.

"All set," he said. "Thanks."

"I've got a couple of packets of pills for you to take with you—pain meds and antibiotics. And a prescription to get more. If anything seems like it's getting worse, you call right away, got that?"

"I'll be fine," Tate said, anxious to leave.

"Quiet and rest. Call me in the morning to let me know how you're doing," the doctor said.

"Will do. Thanks, Doc," Tate said.

He carried his shoes and bundle of wet clothes in his hands, walking in bare feet to Joe's truck ten minutes later, dodging a fretful baby and a harried mother in the waiting room. He winced slightly at the sound of the baby's crying and hoped he'd be all right soon. He hated to see anyone in distress, but right now he just wanted peace from the pounding in his head.

The sun was bright outside. He wished he remembered where his dark glasses were. Probably either broken on the dock or at the bottom of the sea.

"You can drop me at home," he said as he got into the truck. "I don't need to stay at your place."

"Doc's orders," Joe said. "Besides, you might as well have to sit through the wedding preps if Zack and I do."

"Hey, man, this is your big day coming up. You need to celebrate every step of the way." He was happy his friend had found Gillian. Joe's first marriage had ended badly. Tate hoped this one would be forever and Joe would find the happiness he sought. He grew pensive as Joe drove them out of town. He remembered how excited Mandy'd been about their wedding. All he'd wanted was to begin their life together, but he went along with the fancy clothes, flowers galore and sit-down dinner reception. She'd been so beautiful that day. Closing his eyes, he could see every detail. Remember her joy. The plans they'd made. The solemn sharing of their vows in front of all their family and friends. All gone.

Lord, You know how much I miss her! Help me understand why. It was a prayer he often offered.

"I met your tenant today," Tate said to get his mind off the past.

"Faith Stewart?" Joe asked.

"Do you have any others?"

"No. Faith's been in town a few weeks. I thought you vetted all newcomers," Joe said as they left town behind and began the short drive to his house on the bluff overlooking the Atlantic.

"I've noticed her around, but never formally met her," Tate said, gazing out the window. "What do you know about her?"

"Asking as a cop?" Joe drawled.

"Of course. I want to keep Rocky Point safe."

Joe gave him a quick sideways glance as he laughed. "Like Faith could be a criminal element. She's single, twenty-nine, has been a nurse since graduating college. She worked E.R. in Portland. Her credit's outstanding, she likes the apartment but did ask if she could paint the walls and maybe get a pet. I don't know what's wrong with white walls."

"According to Mandy, they're boring," Tate said as casually as he could. He never wanted anyone to forget his sweet wife. It was still hard to talk about her casually. But if he didn't bring her up, others would be too uncomfortable to.

"Faith's pretty, too," Joe said with another glance at Tate.

Tate nodded carefully. The pain had subsided to a dull ache and he didn't want to change that. "Been to church?"

"Me?"

"No, the nurse," Tate said, knowing Joe was yanking his chain. They'd known each other since grade school.

"A couple of times that I've seen. You'd know yourself if you'd been in church the past few weeks."

"Summer's our busiest time. The entire department's working overtime. I've pulled Sundays since I'm the only single guy on the force." He shrugged. "Gives the others time with their families. It'll go back to normal after Labor Day."

"You're okay, you know that?"

"Hey, man, don't get mushy," Tate said and they laughed.

* * *

Faith walked through town as she headed home in the late-afternoon sunshine. Marjorie had been in a huff the rest of the afternoon and she was glad to leave the clinic behind for the day. She wished she knew what she could do to make the woman like her. The only thing that came to mind was her leaving so Marjorie's niece could have the job. And Faith couldn't do that—this was too perfect for her.

"Thank You, Father God," she said softly as she waved at one of their patients walking on the other side of the street. "I feel I've come home here."

She waved to Rachel Sinclair as she passed her antiques shop a minute later, still captivated by the appeal of small town life. She'd stopped in the shop her first week, looking for a small table. The owner had introduced herself and shown Faith what was available. Rachel had talked at some length about Faith's recent move, the history of Rocky Point, the turbulent times during the Great Depression, fishing as an industry and longtime families. Faith hadn't found a table the size she wanted, but had enjoyed visiting with Rachel and learning so much about her adopted town. Rachel said she'd call if and when a suitable table came in.

Faith had made the ice-cream parlor a regular stop on Saturday afternoons. She loved sitting on one of the small tables on the sidewalk while eating a mocha fudge cone and watching tourists wander by. She'd eaten at the café at the other end of town more often than she ate at home. The meals were delicious and reasonable in price. Plus, she liked being around other people and felt a bit lonely when she was home by herself day in and day out. Marcie, who owned the café, had been friendly and even sat with her a time or two while she ate.

As she drew near the sea, Faith inhaled deeply, relishing the tang of salt in the air. Living by the water was good for her. She still didn't have all her strength and energy back—the chemotherapy she'd undergone had sapped so much of that. But today's events proved she could rise to the occasion. Of course, the injured sheriff and the scared toddler didn't quite compare to the trauma events at her Portland hospital. But she'd done well and was proud of making another step toward complete recovery.

And she relished the fact that no one in town knew her medical history. Well, except for Dr. Mallory. No friends hovered over her, watching to see if she was okay. No memories of Allen and his betrayal. No concerned senior nurse cutting back her schedule. Here everyone treated her like a normal person—which she was.

The summer sun lingered in the sky and she swung by the marina park to sit on one of the benches and study the boats tied in slips. Which of the fishing boats on the commercial side had run into Tate Johnson? She wouldn't like to be that guy when Tate was feeling better.

Slowly, the peaceful scene erased the stress from the day. She didn't have many friends yet in her new hometown. It would be nice to have someone to call on the spur of the moment for dinner, talk over what happened during their day. She needed to expand her horizons a little and make more of an effort to forge friendships. She'd spent the few weeks she'd been here getting her apartment just as she wanted it. She still hoped to paint her bedroom, but had put it off. First of all, she'd never done such a project and wasn't sure how to start. And second, most of her free time was still spent resting, or going on walks to build up her stamina.

Time to look to the future and make plans.

Chapter Two

A loud burst of thunder woke Faith up in the middle of the night. She snuggled beneath the covers, glad to be warm and dry. Staring out the window, she watched as two more bolts of lightning lit the sky. The clap of thunder that followed was almost instantaneous. The storm was right overhead. She glanced at the clock on her nightstand. It was almost four in the morning. She'd gone to bed early. Now she wondered if she'd be able to go back to sleep. Staring at the window, she watched as another bolt flashed. Thunder shook the building. Slowly, as the minutes crept by, the storm moved away. She began to relax, drifting.

The shrill sound of her cell phone snapped her awake. She reached over and peered at the caller—Marjorie O'Brien. Was there an emergency?

"Hi, this is Faith," she answered and sat up. If Marjorie was calling in the middle of the night, there must be something wrong.

"Faith. Good thing I found you at home. Dr. Mallory's at the Jarrards—Kathy's in labor and waited too long to get to the clinic or a hospital. So the doc's tied up. It's pouring outside. And black as pitch. Honestly, emergencies should be scheduled better." She sighed in exasperation. "Anyway, you need to get to the clinic. The sheriff called. Apparently there was a mix-up in the medication the doctor ordered for him."

"What kind of mix-up?" Faith asked, concerned.

"He has the antibiotics but there aren't any pain meds and his head's killing him. I think the doctor said he'd written him a prescription and given him some pills to tide him over until he could get the prescription filled. But with all that went on this afternoon, I'm not sure what happened." A hint of accusation filled her voice. "Maybe you got flustered and didn't give all the meds and prescriptions. Anyway, you need to rectify things."

"I gave him the packet the doctor ordered." Faith took a moment to think back. She remembered the envelope with some pills inside, sitting on the prescription sheet.

"The sheriff called the doctor's office and the exchange called me. I'm sure I don't know where the medicine is."

"Okay, I'll go check it out. It'll take me a few minutes. Where do I take the pills?" She was already on her feet, going to the dresser to get something to wear. "I don't know where Joe Kincaid lives."

"Tate said he spent the evening with Kincaids, but then insisted they take him home. His place isn't far from Main Street. Take Kirlandic to Morse and then to Silver. His is the third house on the right. Do you need me to look up his address? Or can you manage that?" The snippy tone in her voice conveyed her disdain to Faith.

"No. I'll figure it out. I'm on my way."

"I'll let him know."

Great, Faith thought a couple of minutes later, it was still pouring rain. Just her luck to be needed during the worst storm she'd seen since arriving in Rocky Point. Her car was parked around the side of the building. Whenever possible she walked around town, to get to know the place and to build up her strength. Dashing thorough the downpour, she reached her car with water already soaking the shoulders of her shirt, dampening her hair, which would make it curl even more tightly.

In only a couple of minutes she was at the clinic. It felt a bit spooky entering the dark building. But once the lights went on, she was fine. She went immediately to the area where sample medicines were kept. Searching for a moment, she saw the packet of pain pills off to one side of the counter, on top of a scrip for more meds, all with Tate's name on them. Faith stared at them for a moment. They had not been there when she left work that evening. Shaking her head, she grabbed them and headed back outside.

The asphalt seemed to absorb her headlights as the rain beat down relentlessly. She had her wipers on high and still had trouble seeing. Carefully following Marjorie's hastily given directions, she had no trouble finding Tate's house. It was the only one on the street with the lights on.

She parked behind his big SUV. Knocking on the door a moment later, she was grateful for the overhang. Though the gusting wind blew rain across the porch, it was not beating directly on her anymore. She shivered. The temperature had dropped noticeably with the storm.

Tate opened the door, his eyes squinting.

"Sorry, I didn't mean to bring anyone out on a night

like this," he said, opening the door wide and gesturing for her to enter. "I thought the doctor would call in a prescription or something and I could get one of the deputies on duty to swing by. Come in out of the rain."

She shook her head to dislodge what drops she could and stepped inside.

"Actually, the storm woke me up before Marjorie called. I thought you were supposed to be somewhere where people could make sure your concussion didn't worsen," she said, holding out the packet of pills.

"I'm fine. Except for the headache."

"Take two right away. It'll ease the pain in less than ten minutes."

"Can I get you something hot to drink before you head out?" he asked, already striding toward the kitchen.

Faith followed, noting the comfortable living room in passing. Big furniture, pictures on the walls, a big-screen television. All softened by a colorful rug, pillows on the sofa and one chair. It looked surprisingly finished for a single man living alone. Had he decorated it himself, or had he had help? She assumed he was single. No one had mentioned a wife.

The kitchen was bright and modern, with stainless-steel appliances, a big double sink and an island where two stools were pushed up against it on one side. The window overlooked the dark backyard. In the distance, flashes of lightning jagged in the sky.

She watched as Tate quickly swallowed the pills. He wore the same clothes he'd left the clinic in. No shoes. Glancing around, she went to the stove and snapped on the light over it, then turned off the overhead light. He swung around and looked at her.

"Easier without that bright light, don't you think?" she asked.

He nodded, then winced. "I hope this headache isn't going to become a permanent part of my life."

"It'll ease up soon. Want me to make something for you? Did you eat dinner?"

"I had dinner at Joe's. I was going to offer you coffee or hot chocolate," he said.

"If you show me where things are, I'll make it while you go sit down in the living room. Leave the lights off—there's enough light from the hall. Rest up for a few minutes, I guarantee the pain will ease up."

It felt odd to be moving around someone else's kitchen, Faith thought a few minutes later as she waited for the milk to heat. It reminded her of spending time in Allen's kitchen. They'd loved to cook together, bumping into each other, and laughing, sharing what they'd done during the day, talking about their future, when they'd marry and make dinner together every night.

She missed that companionship. Missed being loved. Missed being part of a couple. Would she ever have another special guy? Someone who would love her no matter what. Who wouldn't flee in panic if something went wrong. Could she ever trust another person enough to try to build that kind of relationship?

I'm open to anything You have waiting for me, Lord.

When the milk was ready, she prepared two mugs of hot chocolate and carried them into the living room. She'd be taking off soon, but wanted to make sure Tate was feeling better before she left.

Already the sky was lightening in the east. The storm seemed stuck over the sea off Rocky Point. She was in no rush to drive back home in the heavy rain.

Tate lounged in a recliner, his head resting on the back, eyes closed. Quiet though she'd been, he heard her and opened his eyes to look at her.

"Here you go. I hope you like it," she said, handing him a mug. She sat on the sofa opposite the huge television. She'd love to watch some movies on that big screen. It would almost be like going to the theater.

"Thanks. Miserable night to be out," he said, clasping the mug.

"But the rain'll cool things down a bit," she said, taking a small sip of the hot chocolate. Still too hot to drink. "Besides, it was our responsibility to make sure you had all your medicine when you left the clinic." She remembered Marjorie bringing her the small plastic bag with pills and instructions inside.

Had she deliberately left out the pain meds?

Faith tried to ignore her suspicions. She couldn't blame Marjorie for everything that went wrong at the clinic, even though she suspected that Marjorie had a hand in a lot of it recently.

"No problem, except I couldn't sleep, couldn't do anything to get rid of the pounding."

"Feeling better now?" she asked.

"A bit. Not your fault I didn't get all the medication."

"Well, as part of the clinic's team, I'm part of any problem there," Faith said.

He changed the subject. "Where did Marjorie say the doctor was?"

"Delivering a baby at Mrs. Jarrard's."

"Their fifth. I'm sure it'll come fast," he said, taking a drink from the mug. "Umm, this is good."

Faith looked around. On the wall by the front windows were several photographs of a young woman.

She rose and went to look at them. The woman was lovely, with long blond hair and a flawless complexion. She was laughing at the camera in one image, and Faith felt herself smile in return.

"My wife," Tate said, looking at the pictures.

"She's very pretty." Faith wondered where she was when her husband needed her.

"She was. She died a few years back."

"Oh, my. I'm so sorry. She doesn't look very old." Faith was shocked by the knowledge.

"Death doesn't wait for everyone to age," he said.

"No." She thought of her own scare. If the chemo hadn't been successful, she could have died at age twenty-seven. Giving a quick thanks to the Lord for sparing her life, she turned. "You must miss her so much."

"I do. Every single day. We lived in Boston. It was hard to stay there after she died. So when my dad had his stroke, I jumped at the chance to move back home." He sighed heavily. "It's not what I thought I'd be doing at this stage of life, but at least every place I turn I don't see Mandy. Well, except for our furniture. She picked it all out. I couldn't leave that behind." He rubbed the arm of the chair thoughtfully.

"I expect she'd be happy knowing you kept it all. It keeps her alive in your memory."

He looked at her and nodded. "I won't ever forget her. I'll love her all my life. But sometimes it's as if no one around me acknowledges that she lived. That she was such an important part of my life."

Faith went to sit back down. "People don't always know how to handle grief or death. You could let people know you want to talk about her."

He shrugged. "Sometimes I do, sometimes I get so angry she died I can hardly be around people."

"Were you married long?"

"Not long enough. About two years. We'd just begun talking about starting a family when she was diagnosed. Then we spent all we had on trying to make her well."

"How did she die?" she asked, hoping he wouldn't mind.

"Breast cancer. It was awful. She just wasted away. She fought hard, but it was too far gone when it was discovered."

Faith knew nothing she could say would make things better. "I'm so sorry. I'm sure the doctors did all they could." It sounded flat.

"That's what the attending physician said at the hospital. Still, it seems to me that modern medicine should have been able to do something." A shadow crossed his face. "It's so unfair. She was a kind, loving, compassionate woman. She loved being an elementary-school teacher. All her children showed up at the funeral."

"Wow," Faith said softly. Had she died, could she even have counted on Allen showing up?

"Life moves on," Tate said, taking another sip of his drink.

"It does. And it seems to me Rocky Point came out ahead to have you as its sheriff," she murmured. She'd been so devastated when Allen dumped her. But at least he was still alive somewhere in Portland. Their relationship had ended, but both were alive and well. How sad for the sheriff to lose his wife so young.

He gave a slow, lopsided grin and Faith felt her breath catch. His dark eyes seemed mysterious in the dim lighting. But when he smiled, a small dimple peeped out on his left cheek. She looked away before she did something stupid. Like begin to dream more than she should.

"Nice of you to say that. Some days are better than others. But on the other hand, folks around here have long memories and I wasn't exactly a saint when I was a kid. I can't totally escape my past, as I could in Boston."

"So, tell me what awful things you did as a kid," she prodded, intrigued by this side of the sheriff. It must be that the wee small hours invited talk. She was wide-awake and wouldn't be going back to sleep. If talking took his mind off his headache, all the better.

The next half hour or so Tate regaled her with tales of hijinks that had her laughing in utter disbelief. And from the number of pranks he'd managed to pull off, she could tell he'd been quite a terror back then. Yet, all had been done in the spirit of good fun—and without damage to property or people. Some he did alone, most with the Kincaid brothers.

After one account of taking a cow into the high-school principal's office, she asked, "What did your mother do with you after that? She must have been at her wit's end."

"Oh, she and my father wouldn't let me get away with anything, even if they thought the prank was funny. It lost some of its humor to me when Joe and I had to clean up the deposits left by the cow. And take care of the principal's yard all summer long."

She laughed again, then glanced out the window. It was full daylight. Checking her watch, she jumped up. "I have to get going. I'm on duty at the clinic at nine and it's almost seven o'clock now. I didn't mean to stay so long."

He rose and reached for her mug. "Thanks for bringing the pills. They helped. In fact, I'm feeling so much better I'm sure I can sleep for a while."

"Then give me the prescription and I'll have it filled and stop back by after one. That way you'll get some sleep and I'll have the medicine for you when you awaken. The clinic closes early on Saturdays."

"I can get one of the men at the station to pick it up," he said.

"Why bother? I'll be out and about anyway." And it would give her an excuse to check on him in a few hours.

"Okay, thanks."

The rain had settled into a dreary drizzle. The brunt of the storm had moved on over the Atlantic, rendering the sea a steely gray with whitecaps visible as far as she could see. Parking the car in her regular spot at the side of the building, Faith climbed out, vowing to get a sturdy umbrella that afternoon.

She headed for her apartment. Time for a quick shower and breakfast. Hearing a soft, high-pitched squeal, she looked around. Nothing visible. Another two steps and she heard it again, more a mewling sound. Searching around, she saw nothing but wet asphalt and scraggly weeds. She went to the back of the building. There, huddled against the brick wall was a big yellow dog with four little pups snuggled up against her. One was making all the noise, squealing and pushing against his mother.

"Well…hello, there. Did you just deliver those pups?" she asked softly, not going any closer. She looked around. Except for the dog and her puppies, Faith saw no one. "Where did you come from?"

The dog watched her but didn't move. Faith could see signs of delivery, and the tired mother and the wet puppies. The rain had soaked everything.

"I think you need to get them in a warm spot," she said, keeping her voice low. "And you, too, Mama Dog."

The dog wagged her tail and looked at the pups. Faith laughed. "You look surprised to see them," she said, taking a careful step forward. "Where's your home?" she asked softly, drawing closer. "Someone's missing you."

The dog wagged her tail but didn't move. She watched Faith steadily.

"Okay, I'll see what I can find out. Be right back."

Faith hurried back to her apartment. She looked up Animal Control in the phone book, but the closest one was in Monkesville. Hesitating a moment, she called the number listed for T. Johnson, hoping it was Tate's.

He answered.

"I hope you hadn't gone to sleep yet," she said.

"Faith?"

"Yes. I found a mother dog and some just-born puppies. It's raining and I'm afraid the weather isn't good for the dogs. Will Animal Control come out to get them?" She paused to catch her breath. "I saw it's in Monkesville. How early do they open?"

"Yeah, they'll come, but it'd be a while. Can you rig some shelter over them until an officer can get them?"

"Maybe. I didn't get too close, but the dog seemed friendly enough. She's not wearing a collar, or I'd try to find her owner. I don't think she should stay in the rain."

"What kind of dog?"

"Yellow."

"The kind is yellow?" he asked drily.

"No, that's the color, sort of buttery yellow. It's a big dog. I don't know much about breeds."

"Friendly?"

"Seems to be," she replied. "But I didn't get close enough to crowd her."

"Probably a yellow Lab or a golden retriever. Don't know anyone in town who owns one. I can send a deputy."

She shook her head. "Not necessary. I'll see if I can pick up the puppies and bring them inside until Animal Control arrives. If she'll let me, then she'll probably follow and get out of the rain."

"You don't know that dog. She could be very territorial about the pups."

"I'll be careful," she promised. "But I'm not leaving her in the rain. It's cold out there. And puppies are new babies—they need warmth, too."

She put on a long-sleeved sweatshirt and went back into the rain. Her hair was soaked. A hot shower before she went to work was definitely in order. But she couldn't leave the puppies out in this weather. It was decidedly cooler than the day before, and the rain didn't show much sign of abating.

"Hi, Mama Dog," she said when she rounded the corner. The dog wagged her tail, standing and walking the few steps to Faith. Carefully, she let the dog smell her hand, then patted the dog's wet head. "You'll catch a chill out here in this weather. Want me to bring your puppies inside? And you, too, of course? It's warm inside."

The dog wagged her tail and looked back at the puppies. They were huddled together, eyes tightly shut.

"Okay, then." Faith took a breath and went to pick up the first puppy. The mother dog nudged him with her nose. Faith was amazed at how little and light the puppy was. She picked up the others, cradling them all in her arms with no trouble. "Come with me, Mama," she said, walking slowly back to her apartment. The dog walked with her, nosing Faith's arms a few times, as if assuring herself her puppies were all right.

Faith took them right into the kitchen. The linoleum flooring wouldn't be hurt by the dripping water. She ran to get a towel and dried the puppies and the mother dog, settling them on another towel on the kitchen floor.

"I don't have much food for a dog," she said, looking in her cupboards. "You'll take care of your babies, but I need to give you something. You must be exhausted. Probably hungry."

The dog settled with her pups and watched Faith move from the cupboard to the refrigerator. "Do you eat meat?" she asked, looking over. "I have some hot dogs I could cut up for you." She drew the package out, chopped the remaining hot dogs and put them on a plate. Carrying it to the dog, she put in on the floor in front of her. In less than five seconds the meal was gulped. She filled a bowl with water and put it near the dog.

"I guess you liked that. When I go out I'll get you some real dog food." Checking the clock, she rose. "I have to get ready for work, will you be okay here?"

The dog didn't move. Faith brought yesterday's paper and spread it near the dogs in hopes that any accidents would be on the paper.

She quickly showered and checked on the dog and the pups. She dressed and looked in on them again. Drying her hair, she wondered when she should call Animal Control. Maybe later. She'd do it after her shift. They'd be okay until then.

Checking on her furry houseguests once more, she was pleased to see all of them fast asleep. Erecting a kind of barrier by laying her dining chairs sideways across the archway into her small kitchen, she made sure there was plenty of water and reluctantly left for work.

She drove to the clinic, pulling in just before nine. Marjorie and the doctor had not yet arrived, so Faith opened up and prepared the exam rooms for today's patients. She decided not to say anything about Tate's medicines, but knew to double-check on all future patients.

The morning seemed to drag by. She wondered how the dog was doing. Wondered if Tate had gone to sleep, as he'd wanted. Once or twice she thought she saw Marjorie glaring at her, but she ignored the woman.

She mainly wanted to get home to make sure the dog hadn't totally destroyed her apartment. To make sure the puppies were still alive.

Finally, the last patient left. Faith quickly cleaned the exam rooms while Marjorie straightened the waiting room. Dr. Mallory had already left to see patients at the hospital in Portland. When Marjorie was ready to leave, she called out to Faith to lock up. Faith didn't mind a moment to herself. She was sure Marjorie was out to cause trouble and didn't know how to counteract it. She wanted to turn the other cheek, as the Lord had admonished. But she also wanted it to stop! Normally, she got along with everyone she worked with.

Faith went to the drugstore when she left the clinic, and explained about the prescription. The doctor had already called to let the pharmacist know Faith would pick up Tate's prescriptions, so both bottles were waiting for her. She swung by her apartment before going to Tate's. The dog was licking her puppies when Faith rushed in.

"Oh, they're going to be gorgeous," she said, her heart melting at the sight of the baby dogs. The mother looked better now that she was dry.

"I still need to get to the store. Are you okay?" She checked the water bowl and refilled it. "I'll be back soon as I can."

Dashing out again, she drove to Tate's. She knocked gently on the door, not wanting to awaken him if he was still sleeping. But he opened the door a moment later. He'd obviously slept a few hours, for he looked amazingly healthy, except for the bandage on his forehead. He'd also changed clothes—now he was wearing a flannel shirt over jeans. Perfect for the cooler day. Even summers in Maine could get downright cold.

"I brought you the medicine," she said, holding out the bag.

"How's the dog?" he asked, his fingers brushing hers as he took the bag from her.

Faith was startled by the tingling awareness that spiked. She swallowed. She was around patients all the time, touching them, when needed, for assistance. She'd never felt like this before.

She smiled, confused, and stepped back. "She's doing well. I'm going now to get some dog food."

"And Animal Control?"

"Well, actually, I've been thinking about that all morning. I'm sure she's from around here, so it makes more sense to see if her owner comes by rather than have her all the way over in Monkesville." She shrugged carelessly. "I thought I'd keep them a few days, put up posters or something. Maybe she lives near my place and didn't expect the puppies to be born so soon."

He leaned against the doorjamb, studying her. "Or they're so adorable you can't let them go."

Faith laughed. "Okay, so maybe that played a teensy part in the decision. She's really a pretty dog and her puppies are precious."

"Give me a minute and I'll go with you."

"Oh. You don't have to do that. Shouldn't you rest some more?"

"I slept for almost five hours. Took the last of the pain medicine you brought earlier, and I'm feeling almost 100 percent again. Let me get some shoes on."

Faith stepped inside and waited in the living room, going again to study the pictures of Tate's wife. She was so grateful for her own life. How sad that this woman hadn't lived longer.

"Ready?" he asked a moment later from the archway.

She turned and nodded. Her small car was perfectly adequate for her. But once Tate climbed into the passenger seat, it seemed to shrink. She felt self-conscious driving to the store, aware of his every move. Of his watching her.

Once inside the grocery store, Tate was greeted by half a dozen people as they went straight to the pet section. *He must know everyone in town.* It was a bit odd to be stopped so many times to reply to questions of concern. Faith had lived in Portland her entire life and didn't think she knew as many people as they'd run into just at the Rocky Point grocery store.

Tate seemed to know just what to buy, from dog food to bowls to a leash and collar. By the time they were checking out, Faith herself was getting hungry. Should she invite him for lunch? He wanted to see the dog. Maybe he'd recognize the owner and reunite them today.

"Want to pick up something from Marcie's before we head back to your place?" Tate asked, as if reading her mind.

"Does the café do takeout?"

"If we call ahead. We use it a lot when we're on patrol."

Tate had the number in his phone and took care of ordering two shrimp po'boys.

When they reached the apartment later, he brought in the pet supplies, while Faith carried their lunch. The dog barked when they stepped into the apartment, but she didn't leave the kitchen.

"I'm back," Faith called as she went straight into the kitchen, stepping over the makeshift barricade. Tate followed, putting the dog food on the counter.

"Hey, girl. How are you?" He walked slowly toward the new mama dog and stooped down near her. Once she sniffed his hand, he reached out to scratch behind her ears. "Has she been out since you brought her inside?" he asked, looking up at Faith.

"No. I guess she needs to," Faith said, glancing at the scattered newspaper. Still dry. "Do you think she'll run away?"

"Not if her pups're here. They're cute. I believe she's a golden retriever. Maybe a mix. Nice dogs as a rule."

"So someone must own her and be missing her. Maybe they'll walk by when we're out and claim her," Faith said. She had mixed feelings about that. Naturally, she wanted the dog reunited with her owners. But even though the mama dog had only been with Faith for a few hours, Faith would miss her when she was gone.

"I checked in with the station to see if anyone called in about a lost dog after I talked to you earlier. No one has. The dispatcher knows to let me know if someone does," Tate said, standing.

"Well, we'll see what happens." She moved the chairs and went to put the new pink collar on the dog. Once it was on, she snapped on the leash and called the dog to go with her. She came right away and was out like a shot when Faith opened the door, pulling the leash right from her hand. Following more slowly, Faith walked down the stairs to the back and watched as the dog relieved herself. She got close enough to step on the leash, and then took it firmly in hand. The dog pranced around a moment and then ran back toward the steps, looked over her shoulder at Faith and barked twice as she practically dragged Faith to the stairs.

"Okay, okay. That was fast, but I see you need to get back to those babies. I brought you some food," Faith said, running up the steps.

The day had turned surreal a short time later, Faith thought, as she and Tate ate lunch together at her small dining table, where they were able to see the dog and puppies in the kitchen. The last time she'd had anyone over to share a meal had been in Portland just before she moved to Rocky Point. And that had been her friend Helen. Allen had been the last man—gone now two years. Yet it felt natural to have Tate here, discussing the dog and the possibilities for finding her owners.

"I thought I'd take a few pictures of her and post them around town," she said as she slowly ate the delicious po'boy. "If she were my dog, I'd be frantic by now."

"Good idea. If no one replies in a couple of days, we'll expand the area. But I doubt she'd have come far. We can also take her to the vet's and he can scan for a microchip. We might find the owner that way," Tate suggested.

She nodded. "Do you think the owner would be happy enough to have her back to let me have one of the puppies?" she asked.

"You looking to get a dog?"

"I thought about adopting a cat. Joe said a pet would be okay…" She smiled over at the small family. "But I like this dog. I think a dog would provide great companionship."

"A lot of work, too. I had a couple of dogs growing up."

"I never had a pet. So I'm overdue," she said. She looked at Tate. "Any advice about taking care of her until her owners claim her?"

"Watch in case she's not housebroken. Though she seems to be. Feed her according to the directions on the bag. Otherwise, I'd keep the kitchen blocked off so the puppies don't go all over your apartment." He grinned slowly. "Not that they're moving much right now. Probably the owner will claim all of them before long."

Faith nodded, already missing the dogs. She'd never been around puppies before. Who knew how adorable they were? Still, someone was probably frantically looking for her beloved pet. She'd better get going on the posters.

"Why don't you take some digital pictures and then we'll draft the posters on the station's computer."

"Can you do that? I mean, for a dog?"

He nodded. "Why not, this is a missing person—so to speak."

"Are you feeling up to that? You took a nasty crack on the head."

"I'm better than yesterday. I'll take off tomorrow and be back at work on Monday," he said.

"If your headache goes away." She didn't want him to push himself before he was healed.

"Or at least becomes manageable," he said.

She knew better than to argue with a man who was bent on discounting his injury. But she vowed to keep a close eye on him while they were together.

After the dog had eaten, Faith let her out again. Then she took several pictures of the dog, who seemed more than willing to look this way or that as Faith tried to capture the best image. Faith and Tate headed for the sheriff's office in Faith's car.

"I could drive," he said as they left her apartment.

"I'd rather," she said, looking up at him. "I'm not seeing double."

"Neither am I today," he said.

"Still, I think you need to give it another day before driving. Just to make sure," she insisted as she headed the short distance to city hall.

The sheriff's office was smaller than Faith expected. A central room that housed several desks, computers and printers. A counter separated it from the entrance. There were a handful of chairs in the small lobby. Behind the main room was a hallway, with two offices, a break room and a holding cell.

Tate went straight to one of the offices. "Have a seat. We'll make it quick and go put them up."

"If Mama Dog didn't come far, she must live near me. But I don't remember seeing her since I've been here," Faith said. "And I take a lot of walks. Exploring." Building back her stamina. But she didn't have to tell him that.

"She might normally be kept in a backyard from which she somehow escaped," he said as he turned on his computer. In no time copies of the poster were spewing from the color printer. When they had a dozen, he gathered them and stood, grabbing a stapler from his desk.

"Let's go."

The rain had stopped, though the air remained damp and cool. Soon they were walking around the blocks near the water, putting the posters on trees and power poles.

Faith saw a couple reading one just after they put it up. She waited a minute, holding her breath, but they turned and continued on their way. Not the dog's owners.

Tate watched Faith a moment as she waited to see if the couple behind them owned the dog. He saw the relief on her face when they walked on. He hoped she wouldn't get too attached to the dog and be disappointed when the owners showed up.

By the time they'd put up all the posters, Tate's head was starting to pound again.

"I need to head for home," he said as they walked back to her apartment.

"Is your head bothering you?" she asked, immediately solicitous.

"A bit. With little sleep last night, I'm beat. I'll pop back a couple of those pain pills the doc ordered and I'll sleep through the night."

"Come back to my place and I'll fix you something for dinner. Then drive you home. A good night's sleep would be the best thing for you," she suggested.

Tate agreed. Not that he was hungry, but he wasn't in any hurry to end their afternoon together. Faith was easy to be around. She didn't flirt. Didn't try to make a big deal of anything. Didn't seem to expect much. And she was obviously getting attached to her new houseguests. He hoped she'd be all right when the owners claimed the dogs. Maybe she would get one of the puppies out of the situation.

When they entered her apartment, she gestured toward the living room. "Go sit down while I take Mama Dog out for a walk. As soon as we get back, I'll fix us something."

"If it's too much trouble, we could go out somewhere." Not that he wanted to brave Marcie's restaurant. While it was the best place in town, it'd be crowded and noisy on a Saturday night. People would want to check on how he was doing. He didn't think his head could take it. But he didn't want to put Faith out.

"Not a problem at all. I have to eat, too, you know. I'll just be a couple of minutes."

He sat on the sofa in front of a small television. Closing his eyes he tried to relax, but the throbbing in his head was growing stronger. Rising, he went to the kitchen and found where she kept glasses. He took two of the pills he'd put in his pocket before leaving home, watching the puppies as he drank the water. They were so tiny. Hard to believe they'd grow to the size of their mother. Yet he'd been a baby once, and look how tall he was.

Returning to the living room, he glanced around. Sparse on furnishings. Comfortable. Two paintings hung on the wall—both landscapes. One had a cottage in the distance. No photographs. She said she'd been raised in foster care. He leaned back on the sofa and closed his eyes, trying to imagine growing up without his mother or father, his grandparents, Aunt Betty, Aunt Susan, Uncle George and all the cousins. He couldn't do it. They'd always been there for him. Poor Faith, having no family. She should marry and have a bunch of kids to fill the need for family. Then she'd have birthdays to celebrate, holidays for family gatherings. And grandkids to bring her joy in her old age.

The dreams he and Mandy had once had.

Chapter Three

Faith came in a few moments later. The dog ran over to him, sniffed, then took off for the kitchen.

"She's such a good dog. Just does what she needs to do and comes right back. I can't imagine why we haven't heard anything from the owners," Faith said.

"Maybe they're away today and don't yet know she's missing." He started to get up, but she shook her head.

"Stay there. I'll do better in the kitchen without you underfoot." Her smile was teasing, but she could tell from Tate's relieved expression that he was fine with sitting a bit longer. He'd clearly done too much today. That whack on the head must have been worse than they'd thought.

Faith quickly scanned her refrigerator and cupboards, looking for something substantial for dinner. Her choices were pathetic. She had some bacon and eggs, but that didn't seem very substantial for a man of Tate's size. She had cheese and bread. Maybe grilled cheese sandwiches and soup. She had an assortment of hearty soups—her choice when preparing a dinner for one. She'd have to make do.

She fed the dog, petted each of the puppies, then washed her hands and began to prepare the simple meal. When it was ready, she called Tate. He was asleep. She debated letting him rest, but decided that a meal and then rest in his own bed would be best.

"Tate, come eat," she said softly.

"Mandy?" he murmured, still sleeping.

"No, it's Faith. Come eat dinner."

He opened his eyes and looked at her with what Faith was sure was disappointment. He'd been dreaming of his wife. She wished she could have been there for him. She knew how it was to wake up and have to remember reality all over again.

He shook his head slightly, winced and rose. "Didn't mean to conk out on you."

"You must be wiped out. We'll eat and then I'll drive you home. I have to say it's not much," she admitted ruefully, as she led the way to the small table. "I don't usually cook for anyone else and I don't make a lot when it's just me."

"I know about that. I get a lot of my meals out, or at my folks's. When I'm home, a sandwich is about all I eat."

"This isn't much more," she said, feeling apologetic.

"It looks great. And anything I don't have to make is doubly appreciated. Want me to bless the food?"

She nodded, intrigued that he'd offered. The prayer was short, but heartfelt.

After they'd begun the meal, she studied him for a moment. "So you're not a cook?"

"Barbecue—that's my limit. I need food to fuel up...I'm not a gourmet."

"Me, either. But I used to enjoy it."

"Used to?"

She nodded. How much to share? She didn't want people watching her all the time, as her friends in Portland did. She wasn't fragile. She wasn't going to break. Or die any time soon. At least she hoped not.

"I, uh, was engaged a couple of years ago. I loved cooking for the two of us. I'd try new recipes, putting the ones we both liked in a special binder." She still had the binder. Would she ever want to make those meals again? Could she eat any of them without remembering Allen and the promise broken?

"Since you're not married, I'm guessing the engagement ended?" he asked. His eyes met hers and Faith saw the savvy intelligence. Though it wasn't much of a stretch to guess that outcome.

"He broke it off."

"Sorry. Am I sorry?"

"What do you mean?" She looked at him.

"Are you better off without him? Granted, we've known each other a really short time, but it seems to me he was a fool to break it off."

Faith flushed with pleasure at his compliment. "Thank you. That's nice of you to say. Actually, now that I think about it, I'm probably better off. He turned out to be someone who wouldn't be there in good times and bad if we had gotten married. Better to know that before, don't you think?" Over and over she'd told herself that, but in her heart, she still ached that Allen had left at the first sign of trouble. Granted, cancer was a huge thing, but it still hurt.

He shrugged. "I'd say so."

She nodded and continued eating. She knew he wanted to know the entire story, but she wasn't sure she was ready just yet to tell anyone. Truth was, she might never be ready. Still, she had forgiven Allen.

She should explain so Tate would know the full circumstances.

"I had cancer and he panicked and left," she blurted out. Then wished instantly she could snatch back the words. Would it change the way he viewed her? His wife had died of cancer. She didn't want him looking at her and wondering all the time if she was going to end up like his wife.

"Whoa," Tate said, looking at her. He put down the soup spoon. "He just left—when you got sick?"

She nodded. "Promise you won't tell anyone. Dr. Mallory knows, but I don't want anyone else here to know. I got so much sympathy and concern from friends in Portland, I was overwhelmed. Soon everyone saw me as the one who had cancer. As if that was my new identity. Even after all the treatment, when I was cancer-free, they'd be so solicitous." She swallowed hard. "I came here to make a fresh start. I'm two years out and moving on toward five years. Here my identity is new nurse, not cancer patient."

"I don't know what to say." Tate stared at her.

She wished she knew what he was thinking. Would he resent that she'd had cancer and survived when his beloved wife had died?

"You should sympathize with my ex. You know how hard that illness is for loved ones from your wife's death," she said. She didn't want to excuse Allen's betrayal, but, taking a step back, she could see how scary it had been for him.

Tate shrugged. "I couldn't go through something like that again. Watching her slowly go downhill, the valiant way she struggled to stay positive even toward the end when we both knew it was only a matter of weeks, then days. To see her go from healthy to so thin and frail was horrible. Frustrating when all that treatment had no effect." He released a ragged breath. "I hated it! But there was no place else I could be—or wanted to be—but at her side. I loved her."

Faith wished Allen had had that loyalty gene, no matter how hard things got. And as it turned out, she was in remission and maybe even cured. If he had had faith—but that had not been the case.

"Yet you came right away when your father suffered a stroke. It's fortunate he recovered, but what if he hadn't?" she asked. She suspected Tate had depths even he didn't realize.

"Then I would have been doubly needed—for him and for my mother. I'm their only son. Of course I'd be there for them."

"See, you're head and shoulders above Allen. He only wanted things to go along with no major problems. What if we'd gotten married and then I'd been diagnosed? That would have been worse—if he left then. Or grew to hate me because he was tied to me in marriage."

"Maybe he was plain scared," Tate said gruffly.

"So was I. Anyway, that's my sad story. Don't you tell anyone."

"I won't." He was quiet for a few minutes as he continued eating the light dinner.

"There's a happy ending, you know," she said.

"That's right," he replied. "You're cancer-free."

"Well, yes, that. But one of the nurses there brought me a Bible and told me about Jesus's love for me. I'm still learning all I can about the Lord, but I received salvation in the darkest time of my life. It was as if there was a light shining through the darkness and I clung to that."

He nodded. "God is always there. Helping when it suits His plan, comforting when help doesn't come the way we want it."

He meant his wife. "Did your faith waver when your wife died?" she asked. She wanted to stay strong in the Lord forever. But did earthly happenings change that?

He looked up at the ceiling for a moment, then met her eyes. "I was mad, but I don't think my faith wavered. I know the Lord has everything in control. I may not know His plan, but I trust Him."

Faith didn't know whether to regret the confidence or feel relieved. She was glad to hear Tate say his faith remained strong. She wanted hers to be strong forever.

"That's how I feel sometimes. I don't know where I'm going, but I think God has a plan for me," she said. "I'm trying to stay alert so I'll see it."

"I'm sure of it," Tate said.

Faith resumed eating. She would always cherish his first comment about Allen's desertion being his loss. But she knew she'd be watching for any signs that Tate felt sorry for her. Or was watching to see if she was really cured or would have a relapse. That's why she'd left Portland. She didn't want to encounter the same situation here. What she wanted to find was the life God had planned for her.

"What kind of cancer?" he asked a minute later.

"Ovarian. I was lucky. So often that goes undetected until too late. I had the full battery of chemotherapy. I'm still getting over that. But I'm fine." Fine but unable to have children. Fine but wary about falling in love again. How did any of us know before adversity whether our loved ones would stand by us or not?

He nodded, shifting his gaze to the almost-empty soup bowl.

"More soup?" she asked a minute later, hoping the light meal has satisfied him. She was full. There was nothing for dessert, so the sooner she got him home, the sooner he could get some rest.

"No, thanks. That was a nice meal, Faith," he said.

She laughed, "What's nice is your saying that. I don't have a lot of food. Let me put the bowls and plates in the sink and I'll take you home."

Faith dropped Tate at his house and hurried back without waiting for him to get to his front door. He'd asked her in, but she'd refused. She didn't want a lengthy conversation about her health. She was who she was and not the illness that had once haunted her.

The dog barked when she entered and she hurried into the kitchen. For a while she sat on the floor by the dog and talked to her. It was nice to have a companion, even one who just wagged her tail as Faith talked. Once again she hoped the owners would consider letting her have one of the puppies when they were old enough to be adopted. She'd love to have the mama dog, but knew her owner had to be missing her.

Faith took the dog on one last walk for the night and then cleaned up the kitchen. She thought about the sheriff as she put away the dishes, filled the dog's water dish and put down more newspapers for the puppies. She liked being around him. He made her feel more alive than she had in a long time. She liked watching him talk, looking for that dimple when he smiled.

"He's nice. And he didn't freak or become oversolicitous when I told him," she murmured to the dog. She wagged her tail.

"I'll ask around at church tomorrow to see if anyone knows who's missing their sweet dog. Maybe we'll find your family and you can get back home. I'll miss you." She petted the dog and stared into her brown eyes. "I'm glad I found you. What were you thinking, having those puppies in the rain?"

Once in bed, Faith propped herself up to read from the Bible. Saying another prayer of thanksgiving for the woman who had introduced her to the Lord, she let her Bible fall open where it would. She loved the verses from Philippians and reread them for comfort. *Finally, brothers and sisters, whatever is true, whatever is noble, whatever is right, whatever is pure, whatever is lovely, whatever is admirable...* As she drifted to sleep sometime later, she thought again about the afternoon with the sheriff and how he exemplified the verses she'd just read. *Noble* and *admirable* fit Tate Johnson to a T.

The next morning Tate awoke early. The headache was down to a dull pounding. Maybe half the pain meds would do. He'd take today off, and see how he felt in the morning. Calling in to the station, he was reassured to learn that things were quiet. He'd take advantage of the time off to attend the services at Trinity. Maybe he'd see Faith Stewart there.

The day was balmy and breezy. The sun shone in a cloudless sky. Tate drove and parked in the big lot. The neighbors and friends he greeted as he entered were men and women he'd known his entire life. He'd missed that in Boston. He and Mandy had found a church near them, but they were still the newcomers when she became ill. That church had been large and a bit impersonal. Or maybe just in comparison with Trinity.

He nodded to the Kincaids as they met near the double entry doors. Both brothers escorted the women they were going to marry. Joe's daughter, Jenny, stood between him and Gillian.

"Does your head hurt?" she asked, eyeing the bandage.

"Not so much today. Thanks again for helping me out," he said to Joe.

Joe nodded. "Hey, just glad you're okay. Not up to work yet, right?"

"I wanted one more day. The headache's almost gone."

As the group walked up the aisle to the spots where they normally sat, Tate casually scanned the church. Nodding and waving to friends, he didn't see Faith. Either she hadn't yet arrived or she wasn't attending services.

His parents normally sat near the front. He slid into the familiar pew and greeted those already seated. His folks were still away. He knew if his mother had been home, she would have fussed over his injury. The people next to him asked how he was doing. The couple seated behind him nudged his shoulder to get his attention, also wanting an update. It was nice to feel the genuine concern, but the repetition of telling the tale could get old fast.

He had an inkling of understanding of what Faith must have gone through with her friends. He'd thought about her last night. There was a slight reserve about her that intrigued him. He was honored that she'd chosen to tell him about her illness, and her failed engagement. He'd respect her privacy. If she hadn't told him, he would never have guessed. Still, now he knew why she was so thin. He remembered that Mandy'd had no appetite while she was taking chemo. But Faith wasn't going to gain back the weight if she didn't eat more than soup and sandwiches!

Tate couldn't believe the man who had said he loved her would leave her in the lurch like that. All alone, no family and no fiancé to rally around her. Faith had had it hard. Yet she had made light of her sad story. He hoped the people in Rocky Point proved to be better friends if adversity ever came her way.

At the end of the service, he walked out, nodding to friends, speaking to several as everyone moved to the front lawn of the white clapboard church. He spotted the Kincaids and headed their way when several of the teenagers swarmed around him.

"Hey, Sheriff, are you okay?" one of the boys asked as they all stared at the bandage.

"I heard you saved some kid from drowning," another said. "Cool."

"Do you need any help at home?" little Betsy Morgan asked. Her mother was the chair of the ladies' aid team, and he suspected she was going to take after her mother in offering help wherever it was needed in the community.

"I'm going to be 100 percent in another day or two, and yeah, I pulled a child from the water. Make sure you learn how to swim."

The teens laughed and then peppered him with questions, including, Was he still going to play basketball on Tuesday at the high school? They had pickup games every Tuesday during the summer and Tate was always favored to be on a team.

"Don't know about that," he said. "It'll depend on

how my head is. I'll be there, but whether I play or not is up in the air."

"Okay, Sheriff. We'll pray for you. Catch you later!" The teens seemed to move in a swarm wherever they went, he thought, watching them sidle across the lawn, talking and laughing. Good kids, he thought thankfully. And he enjoyed spending time with them. Teenagers, especially, needed to know the adults around them could be counted on to care about them.

Joe beckoned and Tate continued in their direction.

"We're going to Marcie's place for lunch. Want to join us?"

Tate smiled. "Sure." Just then Tate caught sight of Faith talking with a couple near the sidewalk. So she had come to church. Later than he, obviously, since he hadn't seen her before.

"Want to include Faith?" Tate asked on the spur of the moment.

"Sure, the more the merrier," Marcie said. She turned to her fiancé, Zack Kincaid. "Have you met Faith? She's nice…you'll like her."

"Catch you in a minute," Tate said, taking off to join Faith and the Kendalls.

"Hey, Tate, heard you and a boat collided," Josh Kendall said, reaching out to shake hands.

"The boat won," Tate said easily. He smiled at Faith. "Hi," he said. "I didn't see you in church."

"I sat near the back. I saw you right up front," she said.

"We've got to take off," Josh said, looking back and forth from Tate to Faith.

"Good luck finding the dog's owner," Diana Kendall said.

"Thanks," Faith said.

When the Kendalls headed for the parking lot, Tate said, "I'm going to lunch with the Kincaids, want to join us? We're eating at the café."

She thought about it for a moment. Long enough that Tate thought she'd refuse, but then she nodded. "Thanks, that'll be fun. Do you think Mama Dog will be okay until I get home?"

"Probably. You were gone longer yesterday. No one called about her?"

"Not yet. I asked a couple of people today if they knew anyone who had a golden retriever. So far not. Tomorrow on my lunch break I plan to take her to the vet to see if he recognizes her or if she's microchipped. I could understand the owners being gone for a day or two, but not several days, not with her so close to having those puppies. Surely someone should be watching her."

"Maybe we'll come up with other ideas at lunch. My car's right over here. Did you walk?"

"I did. I know, come winter walking won't be as appealing, but as long as the weather's nice, I enjoy the stroll."

As soon as they were all seated at the large round table near the front of the café, Tate announced, "Faith has a houseguest. A golden retriever with four puppies. Any ideas who owns such a dog?"

Jenny's eyes grew large. "Puppies. Can I come see?" She looked at Faith and then at her dad. "Please, I'd love to see the puppies. Maybe I can have one?"

"They're not mine," Faith said, smiling at the girl's sudden enthusiasm. "You can ask the owners when they claim her. I've put up flyers and hope to get a call today. Otherwise I'm taking her to the vet tomorrow. I hope he'll know who she belongs to."

Faith explained how she found the dog and what she'd done so far to try to find the owner.

"You'd think she'd have on a tag or something," Marcie said. "If I had a pet, I'd want it readily identified if it got out of the yard."

"Maybe she did and it came off," Joe said. "I don't remember seeing a golden roaming around." He looked at Jenny. "Any of your friends have a golden retriever?"

She shook her head. "I'll be the first." She almost bounced on her chair.

The adults laughed at her statement.

"Don't count your chickens, honey," her father said. "We have to find the owner first and then we'll see."

She sighed. "That usually means no."

Faith looked at Joe and he winked at her. She knew if he could get Jenny a puppy, he'd do it.

The conversation veered to Tate and his injury, then to the end-of-summer picnic the church would hold at Carlisle Beach, and, of course, the highly anticipated fall football season. Faith was content to sit and listen, though she contributed her thoughts when asked. She enjoyed the lively exchange between the two brothers. And found herself watching Tate more than she should. He was merely a new acquaintance who had kindly included her in a lunchtime gathering of his friends. She was not looking for more. Still, she liked the way he kept the conversation going. The easy manner he had with Jenny. The funny things he'd sometimes say.

By the time everyone had finished eating, the topic of conversation shifted to the upcoming wedding of Joe and Gillian. Faith smiled politely and glanced at her watch. She really didn't want to listen to the excited discussion. Her own plans for a wedding had been shattered. And she was getting worried about how much time Mama Dog had spent without a walk.

Tate caught her eye and tilted his head slightly toward the door. She gave one nod and hoped she was reading him right.

"I've got to head out," he said. "I'll take you home, Faith."

"That would be nice. Thank you for letting me join you for lunch," she said as she got ready to leave.

"If you're going home, can I go with you? I want to see the puppies," Jenny said.

"We'd better wait until we find the owners. Then you'd be able to ask them about having one," Faith said. "I'll tell you what. If no one claims her by tomorrow afternoon, see if your dad will let you come see them. Just keep in mind that they're very small and not moving around a whole bunch," she warned.

"What if the owner never comes?" Jenny asked, her eyes sad at the thought.

"First, let's see what the vet says. I'll be off work at five. You can come and see them after that. But they are very little and I don't know if Mama Dog will let you touch them. She's very protective."

"I'll be very careful. If she doesn't want me to pet them, then I'll just look," Jenny said solemnly.

"Deal." Faith looked at Joe. "Okay?"

"Works for me."

Once in the car, Faith sighed softly. "Thanks for the save. It's not that I don't want others to get married and be happy. It's just hard to listen to the excitement and plans and not remember."

"No thanks necessary. I'm happy for those two. And Zack and Marcie, who will be getting married at

Christmas." He sighed. "But talking about weddings reminds me of mine. Still a bit painful to think about. And I figured you would have the same problem."

"You're right. Maybe one day I'll feel differently."

"Like when you're planning a wedding for yourself."

"I'm not sure I'll ever marry." She wouldn't tell anyone how sad she felt when she thought that. But it would take a special man to want to marry a woman who couldn't have children. Maybe a nice widower who already had children of his own. But then she'd be the stepmother, and that wasn't always a happy situation.

"Why not?" Tate asked.

"Most people think of getting married and having a family. I can't do that." She looked at him. "How will I ever know if I can trust someone? I truly thought my fiancé would stick by me through everything. How wrong I was."

"Not every guy's like that," Tate said.

"True, but how to weed out the ones who are?" she countered.

It took only moments to drive down Main Street. The shops were open, displays in the windows designed to entice buyers. Tourists wandered along the sidewalk. The ice-cream store was crowded. All too soon, the waning summer season would be over. Faith wondered what winter in Rocky Point would be like.

"It's nice here," she said, laughing softly when she saw a rambunctious toddler fleeing his mom, ice cream in hand. "I enjoyed church this morning. Diana Kendall suggested I join the singles group at the church to meet more people. She said it's for confirmed singles—not a euphemism for dating? Is she right?"

"Singles only. All ages—never marrieds, divorced, widowed. About an even mix of men and women. I went a couple of times. Then got too busy. Plus, I already know people in town," Tate said. "It would be a good starting point for you to make friends. Like values and all."

"Want to come in to see the dog?" Faith asked when they reached her apartment.

"Thanks, but I think I'll head on home. Call if you need anything."

"Why, thank you, Sheriff. That's nice of you."

"Tate. Not wearing my official sheriff's hat today. Until the bandage is gone, I don't guess I'll wear the hat at all," he said with a grin.

Faith's gaze flickered to that adorable dimple. She wished he'd come up and stay just a little longer.

"Okay, then, Tate. We'll see you back at the clinic in a week, right?"

"I won't forget," he promised.

Tate watched her run up her stairs and enter the apartment. Pulling away to drive the short distance to his home, he thought about how connected he felt to Faith. Probably because they'd both lost a loved one. He'd just met her two days ago, and yet at the restaurant he could tell she was uncomfortable when the conversation turned to the wedding. She'd gone through some hard times, just as he had. And she seemed to be as wary about marriage as he was. She worried that a mate wouldn't stay true to her. He worried that another woman would become sick and die, and he'd have to deal with that pain again. A fine pair. Yet perhaps because of what they'd gone through, they clicked in some way.

Monday morning was hectic. The puppies were starting to scoot around, eyes still closed—not walking as much as slithering around on the linoleum floor, scrunching up the newspaper she had put down to catch accidents. The mama dog's appetite picked up and Faith was surprised at how much she ate. After taking her outside, Faith was reluctant to leave her home all day. Though Faith fully expected to dash home at lunch, she still worried a bit about leaving the dog on her own.

"I'll be back before you know it," she said as she prepared to leave for work.

The dog wagged her tail.

Checking on the water bowl and fresh newspaper that she'd spread all over the kitchen, Faith finally left.

Hurrying to work, Faith reviewed all she wanted to do today. Take the dog to the vet for a microchip check at lunch. Make sure posters were still up. Ask patients as they came in if they knew the dog. And if no one claimed her before five, Jenny Kincaid was coming to see the puppies. From feeling lonely and at loose ends a few days ago, she sure had a busy schedule today.

The morning flew by. Asking patients casually if they knew about the dog prompted an interest in the puppies and praise for her for taking them on. But no firm idea of who the owners were. Marjorie showed her disapproval when she was asked.

"Take them to Animal Control—that's what they're there for. I wouldn't have a dog messing up my house."

Faith nodded, but bit her tongue to refute the idea. She was not going to take them there, except as a last resort.

She called to schedule a vet appointment, lucky to get in right at noon. Dr. Mallory didn't mind her taking a bit longer for lunch. The visit was disappointing, however. The vet didn't recognize the dog, nor had she been microchipped. He gave her a checkup and recommended that she get a round of shots if the owners didn't claim her soon—just to be on the safe side.

Faith left work early enough to be home at five. Almost on the dot, Jenny and Gillian showed up to see the puppies.

"Come in. They're in the kitchen. I've barricaded them in with my dining chairs, so step over them if you can." Faith continued to keep the dining chairs sideways and overlapped to make a barrier between the kitchen and the living area.

"Oh, they're so little!" Jenny exclaimed when she saw them.

"Move slowly and gently," Gillian admonished. "Let the mama dog sniff your hand and talk to her softly so she'll know you're a friend. She may not want you touching her babies."

Jenny followed the directions and in just moments was sitting by the mama dog holding two of the puppies in her lap. As they squirmed around and tried to settle, she laughed in delight.

Faith and Gillian shared smiles. "They are cute," Gillian said. "I hope the owner wants to part with at least one, since Jenny has her heart set on it. She's talked about nothing else since lunch yesterday. Joe agreed that she could have a puppy if it works out."

"I'm starting to think I may be the one to decide.

I can't imagine where the owners are. Do you want some iced tea while she plays with the puppies? I have a pitcher in the refrigerator."

"Sounds nice. We won't stay long. I know you just got home from work," Gillian said. "I take it you still don't know who the owners are and the vet didn't, either?"

Faith poured two glasses of tea and offered Jenny some juice. Taking their glasses, the women went to sit in the living room.

"It was disappointing that he didn't recognize the dog. But I have to admit I'm sort of glad. It's nice to have her welcoming me home." She shrugged. "And so far, Mama Dog isn't any trouble. The babies are too little to do much, but no doubt they'll be a handful in another week or two."

"A fun handful. No calls on the posters, either?" Gillian asked.

"No. I can't imagine that no one's missing her."

"What did Tate say?"

"That he'd keep an eye out and ask around." She smiled. "But as I said, I'm enjoying the company. And having them around makes me realize how much I want a dog."

"Don't forget you'll have to walk her rain or shine or snow."

"I know." Gillian didn't know that walking the dog would be a great impetus to getting her out, building up her stamina. She didn't see how having a dog could be anything but good. "So...how're the aerobics classes going?"

"My classes aren't disturbing you, are they?" Gillian asked.

"Not at all. I'm not home during the day and your

night classes end early enough not to bother me. I can barely hear the music. I probably should join in, but not just yet."

"Come when you can. I have a long way to go before being full at each session, but the women who do come love it, and we're all having fun."

A few minutes later, Gillian said they had to leave. Jenny was reluctant, but went willingly enough when Faith said she could come to see the puppies again.

Dinner didn't take long to make or eat and, when finished, she took the dog for a walk. Faith had brought the leash, but the dog never wandered far, and if she wasn't on the leash, she couldn't pull Faith. The dog ran around, as if glad to be out of the confines of the kitchen. Finally, she headed for the steps and Faith followed. Just as she started up, a patrol car pulled in beside the building. Tate got out.

"Hi," she called, standing on the bottom step.

He walked over, still in uniform but no hat, just the rakish bandage over part of his forehead.

"How'd it go at the vet's?" he asked, coming to stand by her. He looked up at the dog. "How're you doing, Little Mama?"

The dog barked in welcome and wagged her tail, but didn't leave her spot by the door.

"She probably wants to get back to the kids," Faith said. "Do you want to come in?"

"Maybe for a minute."

"I take it you're feeling better, since you're back on duty," she said as they climbed the steps.

"I took it easy today, mostly paperwork in the office—not my favorite thing. But there wasn't much else to do."

He went to see the puppies and smiled at the arrangement of her chairs. "You should get a kiddie gate to keep them in the kitchen. Be easier on your chairs."

"I could. I just don't know how long they're going to be here. Want some iced tea or something?"

"No, I'm not staying that long. One of my deputies thinks she belongs to a family who was renting a house for the summer. He's contacting the landlord to see if he can put us in touch with the family. They might have just abandoned her."

"What? Why would they do that?" she asked, horrified.

"Who knows? Sometimes people want a pet for the fun factor and when they become work, dump them. They probably knew she was pregnant and didn't want the hassle."

"How awful! How could they do that to her? She's such a sweet dog."

"I don't have a clue why some people do the things they do. Anyway, if we learn who the owners are, we'll contact them," he said. "What if they did abandon her?"

"Can you arrest them?"

Tate laughed. "Unfortunately—no. They should've just turned her in to Animal Control. Which you could still do."

"Not yet." Faith studied the dogs for a moment. "What if the owners don't want her? Can I have her?"

"And the puppies? They'll need shots and a checkup and all before being adoptable. It could end up costing you quite a bit."

"That's not a problem. I still can't believe a family would just dump her to fend for herself—especially when she was pregnant. She's such a love."

"It happens. Anyway, I wanted to let you know we're still looking into it."

"Thanks. Jenny and Gillian were here earlier to see them. Jenny really wants one of the puppies. If it comes to that, I'll find them all good homes," Faith vowed.

"Sell them, recoup some of your expenses," Tate suggested.

"Umm, probably not. Mostly I'd want each of them to have a happy home." She smiled at him. "You look better today. I mean, pain free."

He inclined his head slightly. "And no medicine needed since last night. So I think I am just about recovered."

"What happened to the boat driver that ran into you?" she asked.

"Ah, unhappily for him, he was cited. No way to gloss over it when he slammed into the sheriff."

She laughed. "I expect he'll be cautious from now on. Who would have expected the sheriff in the water?"

"That was his defense—he didn't expect anyone in the water. No excuse for going so fast. The wake alone could damage some of the boats moored in the marina. We'll see if he learned from this." He turned to leave. "I'll let you know if we hear anything about the dog."

"Thanks, Tate. I appreciate it. Now I'll keep my fingers crossed that she can be mine."

He headed out and Faith went to the top of the stairs to watch him. At the bottom he turned and looked up at her. "Do you like sports?"

She shrugged. "As well as anyone, I guess."

"There's a pickup basketball game at the high

school gym on Tuesday nights during the summer. Want to go?"

She was surprised at the invitation. "Who plays?" This was the first she'd heard about basketball games in Rocky Point.

"Mostly teens, but some of them are pretty good. Some of the guys from the church play. Normally, I would, too, but not this week."

"Ah, I'm happy to hear that. Maybe I'll go when you're playing. Thanks for asking."

He gave a short wave and headed to the patrol car.

Faith entered her apartment thoughtfully. It had been a spur-of-the-moment invitation. She couldn't possible read anything into it. It would be a fun activity during the summer. Now, if he were playing, that would be a good reason to go.

Solely to be neighborly, she chided herself. Who was she kidding? She'd love to watch the sheriff play.

Fantasizing about the sheriff playing such an active sport probably wasn't the best thing she could do. She wanted to make a wide group of friends. No romantic entanglements. Which he already knew.

Still, it might have been fun. And who would have suspected the sheriff of playing with a bunch of teenagers? She liked the thought of the men in her new church paying attention to the teens in town. Gave the kids a healthy outlet and they could see men living their walk with God, not just talking about it.

Was there anything for the girls? She'd ask Gillian or Marcie the next time she saw one of them.

The next morning at the clinic, Faith entered, fully intending to make the day a wonderful one. She would be as nice as she knew how to Marjorie and hope the older woman would begin to warm up to her.

By midmorning that resolve was wobbling. Marjorie had been curt to the point of rudeness all morning. Twice Faith had gone to the reception area to call in the next patient and found Marjorie huddled closely with the women patients, talking a mile a minute. About her, she had little doubt.

Show me the way, Father, to get on her good side, please, she prayed.

When she left at lunch to go home to walk the dog and check on the puppies, she prayed the entire walk. She needed some indication of what she could do to make the working situation more harmonious.

Mama Dog was happy to see her, wagging her tail and dying to go outside. Faith laughed. "Okay, but there are going to be some ground rules. You cannot pull me. If I fall, that would be the end of the walks," she scolded as she put on the leash. The dog ran around in circles in her delight. Once Faith opened the door, the dog took off. This time Faith was ready, and as soon as the leash was almost taut, she yanked on it, pulling the dog off her feet. She looked so surprised Faith burst out laughing. "No pulling," she repeated, closing the door. The dog seemed more subdued, but Faith kept a careful hold on the handrail as they descended.

The fresh air and sunshine felt so good. The dog's obvious delight in being outside buoyed Faith's spirits. She was happy.

When she returned to the office, she was in a good mood. Stopping at the reception desk, she picked up the client folders Marjorie had pulled for the afternoon schedule. Underneath them was a pink telephone message slip. Tate had called her and asked him to call back. There was no date or time, but it had to be today.

Marjorie walked in just then.

"Marjorie, when did this call from the sheriff come in?" Faith asked.

"Sometime this morning."

"There's no date or time written in."

"Things get busy," Marjorie said dismissively. "Why is the sheriff calling you?"

"I don't know. I haven't called him back yet." Faith took the message and files and headed back to the small alcove where she had her workstation. She quickly dialed the number Tate had left.

In only a moment, he answered.

"I just got your message," she said. "Anything wrong?"

"Nope. Remember you told me you were invited to the singles group meeting on Wednesday night?"

"Yes, Diana Kendall suggested it. I thought I might give it a try. Sounds like a nice place to meet more people."

"It's a good group. I thought, if you were going, I'd go with you, introduce you around," Tate said.

"Okay. Thanks. How long does it normally last?"

"A couple of hours. There's visiting time, a dessert and then Bible study. I'm sure you'll enjoy it."

When Tate hung up, he smiled. Then frowned. It seemed the friendly thing to do—take her to the meeting and introduce her to the other singles. The members of the group, some of them longtime members, would be welcoming, but it didn't hurt to know at least one person when you were going to a gathering for the first time.

He hoped she wouldn't read anything more into his offer than that of a friend.

He rose. The day was beautiful. He'd spend an hour or so cruising around, checking on things. He wished she'd agreed to come to the basketball game. But he could understand that with her not knowing anyone, she might hesitate to attend. He knew all the kids and the men who played. Had known most of the families his entire life.

Again he thought about how gutsy Faith was to leave the town she grew up in to venture forth into a completely new community and to start a new life.

He'd done that moving to Boston, but he'd always had family and friends behind him, supporting him however they could. He tried to imagine being alone in life.

"Not as long as the Lord is there," he reminded himself as he got into the patrol car. He was glad to know Faith had accepted Christ at her darkest hour. That had to be comforting.

His own walk with the Lord had been shaky for a short time after Mandy died. Then Tate had acknowledged that God was in charge. Tate didn't know the complete plan the Lord had for him, so he accepted the heartache and loss and prayed for the end of grief.

Perhaps it had been in the plan to make the way easier for him to return home, to help his parents, take this job. Maybe even work with kids from church to keep them from getting into trouble. He laughed at that idea. He'd been a rowdy kid himself. Maybe that's why he related so well to some of the restless teens in town. The Lord could take anything and make it to His glory—even Tate's wild past.

He hoped Faith would like the singles group. Maybe, once summer ended, he'd start going again, too.

* * *

Faith smiled when she hung up the phone after talking with Tate.

"Things are looking up," she murmured, opening the first patient's folder to familiarize herself with his medical record.

She began to look forward to the next evening. She'd get to meet new people at the singles group. And the best part was that Tate was taking her.

Which then had her thinking more about the sheriff. He'd looked amazing yesterday in his uniform. There must be some truth to the old adage that men were more appealing in uniform. Though she found him pretty appealing in a T-shirt and jeans. And the flannel shirt he'd worn Saturday. As well as the dress shirt at church.

Oops, too much thinking about him. He was merely one of a bunch of new friends. She knew he didn't intend to fall in love again. Fear of loss kept him wary of any relationship. She felt the same way. After Allen's betrayal, it would be a long time before she was ready to risk her heart again.

Still, it'd be good to have him as a friend.

Wednesday Tate showed up at the clinic at nine. He was seen quickly and the doctor pronounced him almost recovered, except for the stitches that still had another five days to go.

"I know I have to be healing—the stitches itch like crazy," Tate said, winking at Faith as she stood by the doctor's side. She grinned but didn't say anything.

When he was leaving, he asked if she'd walk out with him. Once in the reception area, he stopped. "David, one of my deputies, got hold of the owner of the rental. He confirmed that his summer tenants had a dog. Following up on it, we located the family. They'd had a dog matching the description of Mama Dog, but the husband's saying she ran away." His eyes narrowed. "When David told him she'd been found, with puppies, he stammered and then said they couldn't keep a dog in their apartment and asked if we would take care of it."

"So saying she ran away lets them off the hook? They never even asked about her?" Faith asked incredulously.

"Sometimes people get a dog for the summer. Everything changes when it's back to their normal routine. The dog's better off if that's the kind of folks they are. David had the owner fax over a release and if you still want her, the dog's yours. They called her Maggie." He paused. "She's two years old, not a pure golden, but enough. And they say they don't know who the father of the puppies is. Seeing that they look like their mother, and if they have her gentle disposition, you'll have no trouble finding them homes."

"Oh, Tate, thank you! So she's mine? Maggie. That's a cute name. I appreciate your finding this out for me. I can't wait to tell her."

"Hey, that's what the sheriff's office is for—helping people. And I'm sure Maggie will be delighted with the news." He laughed softly.

"I'm still annoyed they just turned her loose and in the rain and that you can't do anything about it," she said. "There ought to be a law against that."

"Ah, but maybe it's another God thing—your finding her and opening your home to her and her puppies just at the time you were looking for a pet."

She nodded. "Maybe so. I really like her. I'll go home at lunch to tell her she's mine. Thanks." Spontaneously she gave him a quick hug. Then, aware of where they were, of the curious eyes of the patients waiting in the reception area, she backed off. "Thanks again." Turning, Faith quickly went to the back of the clinic. Surely Tate had been hugged before by grateful citizens. She certainly hoped so. What had possessed her to do such a thing? And in public!

Still, she was almost giddy with happiness. Maggie was hers!

Later, when Faith hurried to her apartment at lunch, she wondered again about Tate saying it was a God thing to so easily get the dog. "Did You send Maggie to me, Lord? Am I supposed to have her? She's so sweet and it's nice to have her there when I'm home. I don't know, though. It seems like too small a thing for You to be bothered with."

She passed an older woman on the sidewalk who looked at her quizzically. Faith smiled, realizing she'd murmured her question out aloud. "Lovely day, isn't it?" she said, picking up her pace to escape the embarrassment.

"Maggie?" Faith called when she reached home. The dog jumped the chairs and came running to the door, barking, tail wagging. "So that *is* your name. What a good girl." Faith knelt down to pet her and cooed as she greeted the dog. "Tate said you can be mine. Your other owner's faxing over a paper to make it legal. So once I have that, we can make plans. You need shots and a license and a microchip. If you ever run away, I want to get you back right away. And we'll have to find your puppies good homes." She gave the dog a hug, then stood to go into the kitchen to check on the puppies. It was a small thing to get a pet, but her heart was full.

Tate drove to Faith's apartment that evening. It was warm enough to walk to the church, but he wasn't sure how cool it might be later. Rocky Point was a small, compact town—normally he walked as much as he could. But it wouldn't hurt to drive, just in case. He parked near her steps and checked his watch. He was early. Rolling down the window, he relaxed. *Lord, I hope Your hand's in this. Faith seems really nice and it seems as if she got a bad deal from her fiancé. I hope You bring friends her way. Show her Your love, please, Father, and let her find a place for herself here in town. And me, too, come to think of that.*

He thought he'd live in Boston most of his adult life. But the events of the past several years changed that. He didn't even want to visit, though he did from time to time. Mandy was buried there. There was so much they'd wanted to do together. Would he ever stop wishing things had been different?

Now he was going to a singles group with someone else. He hoped his bringing her wouldn't give rise to speculation. Every time he even spoke to another young woman, his mother thought he'd moved on and was looking to date again. People didn't seem to understand. He knew his parents only wanted him to be happy. Of course, they might also want some grandchildren. He hoped one day he would find someone else to make a life with. But it wouldn't be the same as with Mandy. A shattered heart was hard to make whole again.

Chapter Four

Entering the fellowship hall some time later with Faith, Tate felt self-conscious. It wasn't something he was used to. Men and women he'd known his entire life greeted him. He made introductions and was relieved that no one made a comment about his bringing Faith.

Tate was glad to see everyone warmly greet Faith and quickly draw her into the group. He stepped to the side to watch for a bit. He didn't normally attend and didn't want others to think that had changed.

Pastor John was there to open the meeting in prayer.

"Welcome, Faith," he greeted her. "Everyone, Faith's recently moved to town and works as a nurse in the clinic. Some of you might have met her already. Faith, we hope you'll make a lot of friends here and never want to leave."

She smiled and nodded, glancing at Tate. He nodded back.

"While this is primarily a social gathering of friends, we also have projects we work on together. We're in the planning stage of our upcoming rummage sale, which'll take place in late September. We're forming teams to scour the neighborhoods for donations, then we'll need staffing for that weekend and a cleanup committee. All the money goes to the children's fund."

Tate watched as several members volunteered to head up a team. Then Pastor John looked at him. "What about you, Tate? You know the area better than most."

"Why not? Okay. I'll lead a team." Most of the work for the sale happened after the summer crowd had gone. And he did know the area well.

"Faith, Janette and Peter can work with you. Charlie, how about you? If we have two more teams, we'll be set."

Plans were made for each team to cover different areas, maps were distributed and suggestions for future team meetings were finalized. Conversations were lively the entire time. Then after the group savored a delicious trifle for dessert, the official part of the program began with Bible study, led by Pastor John.

Tate kept an eye on Faith, but he needn't have worried—she was quickly drawn into the group and seemed to be enjoying herself. One of the older men approached him after the meeting ended.

"Say, Tate, you need to do something about those bonfires down on Carlisle Beach at night. They're getting out of hand," he said.

No matter where he went, it was hard to escape being on duty. He discussed the situation with Warren and agreed to have some deputies swing by the rest of the summer to make sure the fires didn't pose a threat. And that the partying that went on didn't get too rowdy.

Faith came over, her face beaming. "I've had such fun. I hope I can remember everyone's name."

Tate introduced her to Warren and then asked if she was ready to leave.

"I am. This was a great idea… I've already met so many people. Pretty soon I'll know everyone in Rocky Point."

He smiled at her enthusiasm. The town and the surrounding area weren't that small.

"And I love the idea of teams foraging for rummage sale items. It'll help me learn about our section and meet even more people. Timing's perfect. So when shall we plan our attack?"

"I'm off next Saturday. Want to grab a bite of lunch at Marcie's and talk about scheduling?"

"With Janette and Peter?"

Tate had not planned to include the other members of their team, but he could hardly tell Faith that. "Sure, I'll check with them."

"Okay. I work until one on Saturdays. I can meet all of you after that."

Tate and Faith sought out Janette and Peter and the four agreed to meet at one-thirty at Marcie's on Saturday.

When Faith said goodbye to Tate a short time later, she ran up the stairs to her apartment, already anticipating seeing him again on Saturday. She was not going to read anything into his offer of lunch, because Janette and Peter would be there, as well. Still, the anticipation couldn't be denied. She liked being with him.

Saturday Faith took a change of clothes to the clinic so she didn't show up at lunch wearing her uniform.

"You must have a hot date after work," Marjorie commented dourly when she saw the change of clothes. "Don't get sidetracked from your responsibilities here."

"Just a group meeting," Faith replied. "I won't let anything interfere with my work here." She was doing her best to keep an even disposition around the woman, but the week had been trying. Marjorie never did anything overtly disruptive, but her snippy comments wore on Faith. She was not going to give Marjorie anything to comment on when it came to her lunch plans.

She hurried to the restaurant as soon as her shift was over. Arriving at the height of the lunch rush, she told the hostess she was meeting the sheriff.

"He arrived a bit ago. He's over there near the window," the hostess pointed out.

Tate sat at a table alone, speaking to a couple at the nearby table.

Faith wound her way through the crowded tables and was pleased that he rose and held out a chair when he saw her. "Am I early?" she asked, glancing at the two empty places.

"Janette called this morning with a cold and bowed out. Peter got a call at work on Thursday and canceled then. So, it's just you and me."

"Oh. Great." She was surprised that Tate would continue with only her. She couldn't contribute much, being so new to the area.

After their orders had been taken, he looked at her. "So, how's Maggie?"

"Doing fine. You'll have to come see the puppies—they're growing so fast. I think they'll open their eyes soon. I can't wait."

"Once they start running around, you're going to have your hands full."

"But what fun!" Faith smiled at Tate, startled to feel a growing awareness around him. His eyes focused only on her. She looked away before he could guess that she felt a mix of anticipation and shyness around him. He was just a friend—that's all.

"So how's your head? Not giving you any more trouble?" She needed something to take her mind off her attraction to the sheriff. She would be horrified if he suspected.

"No trouble for days now. Good as new. I hoped to get the stitches out before my mother saw me, but Doc said to come in next Monday. She and my dad'll be home Monday, so it's a question of timing."

"You haven't told them about the accident?" Faith asked.

"Not yet. Once they're home I'll fill them in. But I didn't want to worry them on their trip." He scrubbed a hand across his jaw. "They rarely leave town, rarely take time off. I think my dad's stroke's given them a different perspective on things. If it had been more serious, I'd have called."

"Did you tell me your father owns the hardware store?"

"He does. I used to work there as a teenager. One reason I bought a house is to fix it up. Not much time during the summer months to work on it, but once the tourists leave, this town really gets quiet. That's when I can get a lot accomplished."

"I think it's quiet already. Work is nothing like the E.R. in Portland."

"Tell me more about Portland," Tate invited.

Faith talked about her job and the friends she had

made at the hospital. She carefully omitted any mention of Allen. She was doing her best to move on from that stage of her life. The conversation moved to Tate's time in Boston and comparisons of the two cities.

By the time they finished lunch, the café was almost deserted.

Faith glanced around. "Did we run everyone else off?" she asked.

"Lunch's over and there are other attractions on one of the last Saturdays of summer. Another couple of weeks and we'll have the headache of Labor Day weekend."

"And that's a headache why?" she asked.

"Kids go crazy. Blowing off steam, trying to cram everything they didn't get done all summer long into three days. Others are leaving and want one blow out weekend to remember. Everyone in my department's on duty that weekend. Clinic, too."

"Good to be forewarned. Dr. Mallory said something about being available that weekend." She returned to the task at hand. "Do you still want to go requesting donations, since it's only you and me?"

"Of course. We'll get a head start on the other two."

She grinned. "So if you weren't here, what would you be doing today?"

"Probably painting the back bedroom in my house."

"Umm, I want to paint the bedroom in the apartment—Joe said I could. But so far, I haven't had enough energy. It'll be a project for fall."

"It goes easier with more than one doing the work. You should have a painting party."

"Invite people over and expect them to work?" she asked.

"Why not? People have been helping others out for centuries. Remember hearing about barn raisings?"

She nodded. "In history lessons. Hmm. Have you ever heard of painting parties?"

He shook his head. "Can't say that I have. I like the mindless work, the time to think while I'm making a change to the house. Couldn't do that if there were a lot of people around."

"Do you plan to live there forever?" Faith had never owned a home and wondered how it would feel. She wanted to put down roots—but could she commit to such a huge purchase one day?

"No. I'm hoping to sell it when I'm finished. Move on to another place and fix it up. Gives me something to do. It's a family home, three bedrooms and two baths, big yard. Not meant for a single man."

She grew thoughtful. From the little she'd seen, Tate would make a wonderful family man. She hoped one day he'd find someone to love again and maybe have that family.

Marcie Winter came over to their table, grinned and sat down in one of the empty chairs.

"Hello, you two. What's up?"

"We're planning for the rummage sale," Tate said.

"Oh, I have a bunch of stuff. Am I on your route?"

"No, we're out by the Fullers'," Tate said.

She wrinkled her nose. "Whoever's covering the town, tell them I have some things I don't want to move out to the house when I get married. Might as well get rid of them now as later."

"I think George is heading up that team," Tate said. "I'll let him know to check in here since you're so rarely home."

She grinned and gave a little dance move in her

chair. "I know. And come December, I'll be living out in a house with a white picket fence."

Tate nodded, glancing at Faith. "Marcie and Zack are going to live in the Kincaid family home. Joe and Jenny are moving to Gillian's house when they get married."

Marcie looked at Faith. "How're the dog and puppies?"

"Doing well. The puppies are growing like crazy."

"I heard you're officially the owner now," Marcie said.

Faith nodded, growing used to news traveling fast in the small town. "Want a puppy in a few weeks?"

Marcie chuckled. "No, thanks. I'll hold off on that. But I know Jenny's dying to see them again." She looked back at Tate. "You should invite Faith to the wedding."

"Isn't that the bride's prerogative?" he asked.

"You can bring a date," Marcie said.

"Not practical being in the wedding party," he responded.

Faith knew the last thing Tate wanted was anyone pairing him up. "It's on a Saturday, right? I work Saturdays," she said, hoping to smooth things over.

Marcie shrugged. "Just a thought."

"We have work to do," Tate said. "Unless you want to join our team to forage for donations?"

Marcie laughed and rose. "I no longer consider myself single, now that I'm engaged. You two have fun." She smiled and left, stopping at another table to talk to that couple. The staff was busy clearing tables and setting things up for the evening meal.

"Never trust a newly engaged woman. Now she wants to do matchmaking," Tate grumbled.

"She's met her match in us. We're immune," Faith said as they rose.

"True enough. Come on, let's get out of here." He paid the tab and they walked out to the parking lot. "I thought we'd drive to the outlying area first and stop at some of the homes on our route to let people know we'll be coming back in a few weeks to take anything they're donating."

Tate had his own SUV today, not a sheriff's car. Soon they were heading out of town to the outlying homes of the community. Faith enjoyed the drive as the road wound among trees and open areas gave a view of the sea.

"This'll be a good chance for you to meet more people, plus give me a chance to talk to them, as well," Tate said as he slowly drove up to a house.

"Don't you talk to them when you see them in town?" she asked.

"If I run into them. Being a cop here's a lot different than in Boston. The city's too big to get to know the majority of residents in different areas. Here, I like to keep track of what's going on, who's doing what. And make sure everyone knows I'm available anytime."

She nodded, thinking about Portland. She had only known a few police officers—the ones who had showed up in the E.R. with an accident victim or a suspect. In her old apartment, she didn't even know where the closest police station was. She'd been in Rocky Point less than two months and she'd already visited city hall and seen the sheriff's office.

"That's one of the reasons I moved here. I wanted the small-town closeness. Portland isn't as big as Boston, but it can still be impersonal," she said, already hopeful about meeting more residents.

Tate came to a stop by a saltbox house surrounded by old trees. A small black dog with three white paws came running from the back, barking, tail wagging.

"This is the Comstalks' home. They're a young couple with two kids," Tate said, getting out. Faith climbed down, smiling at the dog as it came dancing over, tail wagging so hard it almost knocked him over.

"Hi, there," she said, letting it sniff her hand and then patting it.

A young woman came to the door. "Hi, Tate. Socks is better than a doorbell. Come on in."

"Marylou, I'd like you to meet Faith Stewart. She's the new nurse at the clinic. And on the rummage sale committee this year."

"Whoa, you must be a newcomer…that's one of the busiest committees at the church. That and the Christmas pageant. Don't get on that one if you want any free time between Thanksgiving and Christmas. Come on in. I can make some coffee," Marylou said.

"Thanks, we won't stay long. This is your friendly reminder that we need items for the sale," Tate said, holding the door for Faith then following the two women into the living room.

Faith liked Marylou and her warm welcome. "Have you done the rummage sale before?" Faith asked.

"Never been on the committee, but my mom's been involved for years and always enlists help from me and Sam before it's over. I can talk from experience about the Christmas pageant. That one I have been on."

"And you volunteer every year," Tate said as they all sat.

"Well…" She shrugged, smiling. "When did you move to Rocky Point, Faith? Have I seen you in church?"

"I moved here a couple of months ago and I've been attending Trinity."

"And already involved—good for you. The Lord loves willing volunteers. We're lucky you've jumped right in."

Faith smiled and nodded. She couldn't claim too much credit, though. Tate had talked her into going to the singles meeting and that led to her joining the committee.

They chatted for a while, then Marylou gave a quick rundown of the items they could expect from her. Tate jotted them down in a notebook. "So you don't need us to pick up, right? Sam can bring all that in his truck."

"Yep, count on us doing that. So nice to meet you, Faith. I'll see you Sunday."

The afternoon went smoothly. There was someone home at every place they stopped, and Faith met couples, older men and women, young children. Her head was spinning by the time Tate returned her to her apartment. She was tired, but felt buoyed up from all the positive responses to requests for donations to the annual sale.

"That was fun," she said, checking the notes Tate had taken about who was donating what. "I think I need to study names and donations, so I can recognize all of them next time I see them."

"Take your time. Most of us aren't going anywhere."

"Want to come up and see the puppies?" she asked.

"Sure." He grinned at her and Faith felt her heart flip over. Her tiredness fled. She smiled back and hurried from the car, admonishing herself that he was merely being neighborly. He didn't want any involvement of a romantic nature, nor did she. So he was drop-dead gorgeous. She'd seen gorgeous men before and never felt her heart tumble. So what that the dimple in his cheek cried out for her to touch it. She could never let herself get carried away. Taking a deep breath, she vowed to get a grip on her emotions.

But for the moment, it didn't seem as if the rest of her was keeping up with her resolve. She loved spending time with him. Liked the feelings of excitement that stayed right on the edge when he was around. He was funny and smart and she was pleased that he treated her as if she were an old friend. He hadn't brought up her confession about her disease, taking her at her word that she was fine. No hovering over her, no watching her when he thought she wasn't looking.

No more tiptoeing around, for which she was grateful.

"Let me call in just to make sure things are okay," he said as they walked up the stairs.

"I need to take Maggie for a walk—we'll be quick. You can play with the puppies while we're out."

In only ten minutes Faith was back in the apartment. Tate was sitting on the kitchen floor, teasing one of the puppies with a bit of torn newspaper. Their eyes were open now and they tried to walk around, slipping on the linoleum, scrambling over his legs, running to their mother.

"Aren't they sweet?" she said, sitting next to him and reaching for one. Her fingers brushed against his and she tried to ignore the spark that seemed to flare between them.

"I heard that Jenny Kincaid's in love with them all," he said.

"Nice if Joe would take them all," she quipped.

Tate laughed. "He has enough on his plate with

moving and marriage. One dog will be a nice addition to the family."

"Umm, know anyone else who might want one?"

"I'll take some pictures and we'll post them in the library, down at the station and in the grocery store. I'm sure you'll have them all placed before the week's out."

"Nothing critical at work, I take it," she said a few minutes later as they both placed the puppies next to their mother and rose.

"Nope, deputies report everything's quiet. When it gets hectic is later, after the bars have closed and some people don't want to end the party. If they take it to Carlisle Beach south of town, we keep an eye on things." He looked over at her. "But some want to party at the park near the marina, bringing beer or strong liquor. That's not allowed. We try just to move them along. Sometimes people get belligerent."

"Still has to be safer than some of the neighborhoods in Boston," she said.

"True. And once summer visitors leave, things really get quiet. It helps that everyone knows everyone else. Can't get away with much."

"Umm." And one day, she'd know most of the people in town.

"Do you want to stay for dinner?" she asked, glancing at the clock. It was getting to be that time and she was hungry.

"You fed me before. How about we get some steaks at the store and cook them on my grill. If it stays warm enough, we can even eat out on the deck."

Faith smiled. "I'd like that. Let me feed Maggie, take her out again and then I'll be ready to go." She couldn't help being pleased that Tate didn't want to end their afternoon together. And she looked forward to seeing more of his house and backyard.

Faith noticed several curious glances when they were shopping at the grocery store. Several people greeted Tate and he, in turn, introduced Faith. It felt odd. In the past she had never run into anyone she knew at a store. From the glances between the others, she knew they were speculating on the two of them being together. She looked at Tate. Did he care if people thought they were seeing each other?

They were—but only in a friendly kind of way. Maybe she was making a mistake in doing things with him. She already looked forward to seeing him more and more. She had to make sure she kept her emotions under control. No falling for the handsome sheriff. He was no more interested in starting a relationship than she was.

When Tate pulled into his garage, they entered the house through the side door straight into the kitchen. Tall cabinets lined the walls over the spacious counters. The modern appliances gleamed in the overhead light. A door in the back led directly to a deck, which gave way to a grassy yard surrounded by trees.

"This is nice," she said, wishing she had some outdoor space. A balcony or deck would be perfect.

"I like it. In Boston, we didn't have anything like this. Sometimes we'd take a picnic to a park, but longed for the time we could afford a larger apartment that had a balcony." He grew silent, looked pensive.

Faith knew he regretted that what he and his wife had planned never came to be. She shared that kind of regret from time to time. She'd always thought she and

Allen would make the perfect marriage. How wrong could a person be?

"What can I do to help?" she asked gently.

He looked over and smiled. "Want to wash the potatoes? We'll get them baking once I get the grill fired up."

It wasn't the same as working in the kitchen with Allen, but it was pleasant, Faith thought as she scrubbed the baking potatoes and put them in the tinfoil to snuggle in the coals. Tate seasoned the steaks and put them in the refrigerator until it was time to cook.

"I have iced tea or lemonade or soda—what's your preference?" he asked when all was ready.

Faith chose lemonade and took her glass out on the deck. It was a bit cool and she was glad she'd worn a sweater over her T-shirt. Several Adirondack chairs on the deck beckoned. She sat down and relaxed. The peaceful deck was a pleasure. She'd enjoyed the day and was glad it wasn't yet over.

Tate joined her, sitting on the next chair.

"I built the deck," he said.

"It's nice. Do you use it often?"

"Not as much as I thought I would. Usually I grab dinner at Marcie's café or take something to eat at the office."

"I think if I had a deck like this, I'd eat outside every day the weather permitted. And you have all this privacy with the trees. I know you have neighbors, but you can't even see them."

"You can hear them, though. Frasers on the right have teenagers who love to blare their music when they're home. But, in all, the house's in a good location."

When it was time to grill the steaks, Faith found plates and utensils and set the round glass table on the deck. There was no breeze, and the ambient temperature hadn't dropped much, so it was still comfortable to remain outside.

Just as dinner was finished, Tate's phone rang. He rose and went into the kitchen to answer it while Faith stacked their dishes and carried them inside.

"I'll be right there," he said, as she placed them in the sink. Hanging up, he turned to Faith. "I've got to go. There's been an altercation, gunshots fired," he said, hanging up the phone. "Leave those and I'll take you home first."

"Or I can walk. It's not that far and still daylight out."

"Nope, you're almost on my way, so I'll take you home. Come on." He hurried down the hall and returned a moment later wearing a sheriff's shirt, badge and gun.

He drove his own car and soon stopped in front of her building. "Sorry I can't walk you up," he said, a hint of impatience showing.

"I'm fine, Tate. Take care." She hopped out and watch as his car took off, turning the corner almost on two wheels. So much for their quiet evening. She hoped it was nothing serious. But of course it was, or they wouldn't have called him on his day off.

"Please, Lord, bless Tate and keep him safe," she murmured. She looked up to the sky, wondering what the Lord's plans were for her future. "Thank You for a wonderful day," she added.

Tate drew up in the middle of the melee. Two deputies looked like they'd been in the thick of the scuffle.

One man sat on the curb, hands in cuffs, holding a handkerchief to his bleeding nose. Another was cuffed to one of the support posts for the overhang of Rachel's antiques store, yelling at the man the deputies were still trying to subdue. The front window of the store lay in shattered shards on the sidewalk. The third man was being held back by Tate's deputy, Jason. That man kept lunging toward the one by the post.

"What's going on here?" Tate asked.

"Drunk and disorderly, aggravated assault," Jason said, restraining the man once more. "Stay away from them! We need your cuffs, Sheriff, we used ours. This bozo had a gun and shot out the window."

"Hey, I was aiming at him, missed and got the window by mistake," the man complained.

"Lucky for you," Tate murmured, taking his cuffs and handing them to the deputy. "Are you dumb as a stick or drunk out of your mind? We don't allow guns in town. Don't you see people out walking around? What if you'd killed someone? There are kids at the ice-cream shop."

"Aw, I wasn't aiming at no strangers."

Tate shook his head.

In a moment the man was subdued and Tate got an abbreviated version of the situation. "So no one shot." Looking at the one on the curb with the bloody nose, he asked "What's the story with him?"

"Punched in the nose."

"Anyone call the doctor?" he asked.

"He's not on duty tonight and the on-call doc asked if we could get the nurse to assess the damage. If this guy doesn't need a doctor, he doesn't want to come here from Monkesville."

Tate had let Faith off too soon. He asked the other

deputy to call the clinic to see if Marjorie could contact Faith. He had her phone number, but at his house.

"I'll take him to the clinic. Take these other two to the jail. We'll sort through everything there. Book that gun into evidence," Tate said, going to the injured man. "Did anyone call Rachel?"

"Will do," Jason said.

"Hey, he still owes me a hundred bucks," the most belligerent man shouted. "I want my money."

"I don't owe you nothing!" the one by the post retaliated.

"You two can iron all that out later. Right now we want to clear the street," Tate said, going over to the deputy. "Ask someone here to keep an eye on the store until Rachel shows up. Get these two over to the jail." He hoped the injured man wouldn't bleed all over his SUV. He hadn't had time to swing by the station to get a patrol car.

They arrived at the clinic a minute later. Tate had the man out and waiting by the door when Faith drove up a few moments later.

"Sorry to bring you out for this, but the doctor on call wanted your assessment before coming over from Monkesville," Tate said.

"Rightly so. On first glance it looks like a bloody nose. Come on in." She unlocked the door, flipped on the lights and moved directly back to exam room one. She worked efficiently to clean the blood from the man's face, assess that the bloody nose was the source of the blood, though there were bruises already showing around his eyes.

"Tip your head back and hold this," she said, pressing a cold compress against his nose. "What happened?" she asked Tate.

"Fight on Main Street. We're lucky it wasn't worse, one of the men had a gun and shot out Rachel's shop window," he said. "Good thing he didn't kill anyone." He stood near the door, watching Faith take care of the man. She had a grace about her that fascinated him. She was totally caught up in treating her patient. He'd had mixed emotions all evening. Sometimes being with her felt like a date. And then he'd want to pull back. Yet she'd never flirted or made any insinuations that she saw their relationship as more than just platonic. Still, he hadn't had anyone to his place to eat before and hoped she didn't read more into that than he meant.

He'd have a better handle on her feelings if they hadn't had to end their dinner so abruptly. Would she have stayed to help with dishes, or insisted on being taken straight home?

Should he say anything or just let it ride? He'd spent more time with Faith today than with anyone in a long time. Only because they were on the rummage sale team and the other team members had not joined them. It was nothing more than that.

"Poor Rachel. But I'm glad no one was hurt."

"Hey, I'm someone," the man on the table said indignantly.

"Mmm. I think your guy's good to go," she said. "I'll let the doctor know he's not needed on this."

She reached into a cabinet and took a handful of gauze packets, offering them to the injured man. "I'm giving you some pads to take with you in case it starts bleeding again. And I'd suggest you wash that blood out of your shirt with cold water as soon as you can."

"Which won't be before you're booked at the jail and someone responsible can come for you," Tate said.

"Thanks, Faith. I appreciate this. Bill the sheriff's department."

"Will do."

Tate drove straight to the sheriff's office to sort out the fracas. All three men were charged with disorderly conduct. The one with the gun had an added charge. After checking with the police in their respective hometowns, each was released on his own recognizance, with strict orders not to get into another altercation in his town. They'd have to come back to Rocky Point for their court dates.

Tate waited until the officers had finished their written report before heading back home. His evening was shot, so he might as well check out what had gone on during his day off.

By the time he returned home, it was dark. He finished clearing the deck, did the dishes and went to the living room, thinking he'd watch some television. Instead, he glanced at Mandy's photos, as he often did. Giving in to impulse, he veered over to study them. He smiled, looking at her—she'd brought him such joy. She'd been so alive. These were taken before she began to waste away from the illness. She'd insisted he remember her as she'd been, not as she was in her last days.

"I miss you," he said softly, reaching out to touch the cold glass. He would always miss her. Sometimes it seemed like a dream. They'd met, fallen in love, married and she'd died. All within a few years. Those last months had been the hardest he'd ever lived through. But he couldn't have let her down. She'd meant too much to him.

Sighing for the future they'd both lost, he turned and went to the sofa, sank down and turned on the TV.

Tomorrow it was back to work. His parents were due home Monday. Stitches due out. And he wanted to see Faith again.

Whoa, where had that thought come from? He'd decided earlier to cool things between them. No sense in giving her the wrong impression. She'd been hurt enough by one man. Tate didn't plan to be another.

But try as he could to get engrossed in the TV sitcom, his thoughts returned to their afternoon together—visiting, playing with the puppies, dinner. He'd enjoyed the day more than any other in a long time. So what did that mean?

Would she be in church in the morning? If things were quiet, he could stop in for the service. It would only be polite to say hi and ask about the dogs. Maybe update her on the three men who had abruptly ended their evening together.

Restless, he rose, switched off the TV and went out on the back deck. "Lord, I could use some guidance here, please." The silence of the night seemed to seep into him. Peaceful and serene, he studied the stars in the sky. He didn't want to get involved with anyone, but friends hung out together. It didn't have to mean anything more. As long as they were both clear on that.

Chapter Five

Faith's experience at church the next morning was completely different from her earlier attendance. She recognized Rachel from the antiques shop and greeted her, commiserating on the damage to her shop. Then two members of the singles group came over to say hi. She saw Marylou and waved as if they were old friends. She felt more connected than ever and it was a great feeling. Janette entered behind her and came over.

"How's your cold?" Faith asked.

"Now I'm thinking it's some kind of allergy. I feel fine, but keep sneezing and coughing," she said. Then she sneezed.

"Bless you," Faith murmured.

"Where's Tate?" Janette asked, looking around.

"I haven't seen him today. I think he's working."

"Umm, he misses a lot of Sundays in the summer due to work. Want to sit together?"

"I'd like that," Faith said. Janette waved to another couple and then called a hello to another member of the singles group. They walked into the sanctuary and headed to the middle.

"This okay?" Janette asked, slipping into the pew.

"I have no preference," Faith said, sitting beside her. She looked around, already feeling comfort and peace seep into her. She saw the Kincaids near the front on the left side. Striving to be casual about her perusal, she looked for Tate. She tried not to be disappointed when she didn't see him.

The music was familiar and she enjoyed singing the old hymns. Pastor John's message about trusting God seemed to be directed to her. She listened attentively and hoped she could remember the points he made. When he referenced a passage in the Bible, she made a mental note to look it up. She was trusting God to direct her path. She just wished sometimes He'd give her a glimpse of what lay ahead.

When the service ended, Janette invited her to lunch.

"I'd love to. Is that a tradition here, going to Marcie's after church? Last week I went with the Kincaids." And with Tate.

"For a lot of us. We'll see others from Trinity there. Especially in the summer. Sometimes we pack the terrace."

They made their way to the back and out the double doors to the front lawn, where groups of people gathered to visit. Faith felt more a part of the community now that she recognized people she'd met. Then she spotted Tate. He was wearing his uniform, without the utility belt or gun. He stood with the Kincaids and an older couple. Were they his parents? If so, they'd come home a day early. How had his mother taken his injury?

She looked away before he could catch her staring at their group.

"So will others from the singles group be joining us?" Faith asked Janette, turning slightly to make sure she didn't give in to temptation and look at Tate again.

"I expect so. We'll see when we get there. Did you drive or do you want to walk over?"

"I walked this morning. I really like that aspect of living in Rocky Point—I can walk everywhere."

She and Janette started down the wide walkway toward the sidewalk. Faith longed to glance just once more in Tate's direction, but resisted.

"Faith!" a young voice called.

She turned at that, her eyes going directly to Tate, who was looking right at her. Her heart fluttered slightly and she shifted her gaze to Jenny, running over toward her with two friends.

"Faith, can we come see the puppies? These are my friends, Sally Anne and Melissa. They want to see them, too. Maybe Melissa's mom will let her have one. I get first pick—don't forget."

"Hi," Faith said, smiling at the excitement of the young girls. "I'm going out for lunch but will be home later if you want to come by then. I'm sure the puppies would love to see you. They have their eyes open now and are starting to scramble around. You'll love them."

"I already do," Jenny said. "What time should I tell my dad to bring us?"

"How about three?"

"'Kay, thanks." They ran back to the group where Tate stood. Faith looked up once more and smiled, then turned to rejoin Janette.

"Puppies?"

"Oh, my, let me tell you about my puppies…" Faith said.

Lunch on the terrace of Marcie's café turned out to be fun. There were others there from the singles group and they pushed two tables together. Everyone reminded Faith who they were and then when Janette mentioned the puppies, that became the first topic of discussion, which segued into tales of dogs owned in the past.

The sun was blocked by patio umbrellas. The slight breeze from the ocean kept the temperature comfortable. The food was fabulous. Faith was reluctant to leave when lunch was finished. She didn't think she'd ever laughed so much at one time in her life.

"See you Wednesday" was the common goodbye. She was glad to join in with the same farewell. She did have Wednesdays to look forward to.

"Bring Tate again," someone called.

She smiled and waved. As if she had any say over what the sheriff did.

As soon as she reached home and changed, she took Maggie out for a run. The mother dog was flourishing and seemed glad to get away from the puppies for a bit. Faith liked having the dog with her on walks and today on a short run. She was winded before long, but the fact that she could run at all showed she was getting back her normal stamina.

They stopped at the park by the marina and Faith sat on one of the picnic benches. Two other picnic tables had families still enjoying their lunch. Maggie sat beside her, tongue hanging out, content to stop for a moment.

It's so beautiful here, Lord, Faith thought. *Thank You for bringing me here. I couldn't have found a better place to start this new stage of my life. And I want to trust You better. I think the pastor's message was especially for me. Please, let me feel Your love that's there for me.*

She heard a car stop behind her and looked over her shoulder. Tate was getting out of a police vehicle. He waved and she rose and went to meet him, Maggie pulling on the leash in her excitement to see him.

"Hi," she said. Suddenly the day seemed even brighter.

"Enjoying the sunshine?" he asked, stooping to give the dog a greeting.

"Maggie and I had a short run. Now it's time to get home. We're expecting visitors."

"So I heard, when Jenny came back full of excitement. Little girls adore puppies. She thinks her friend Melissa will ask for one, too."

"Maybe. I need to hear from Melissa's parents first." Suddenly Faith felt shy. Her smile felt awkward and she was uncertain of what to say next. She couldn't help remembering the last comment at lunch—"Bring Tate to the next singles group meeting." "Are you on patrol?" she asked.

"I am. I saw you and Maggie and thought I'd stop. Usually it's quiet on Sundays, but it doesn't hurt to keep a visible presence."

"Umm. Not so quiet last night. What happened there?"

"An altercation over a loan one made to the other. Their buddy tried to referee and got a bloody nose for his trouble. All have been booked and released. Let the court sort out the next stage. I saw you heading out with Janette after church. Did you two have lunch together?"

"We did, along with Stan, Mollie, Peter, Seth and Dana from the singles group. I think I have everyone matched to faces. I'll see them Wednesday. They said they hope you come again."

He studied her for a moment. "'Bring Tate,'" he guessed.

She laughed and nodded. "As if I could influence you in any way."

"If things are quiet, I'll go again. Want me to pick you up?"

She looked up at him. "Actually, if the weather's nice, I'll walk."

"If it rains, I'll pick you up."

"Okay. Thanks. Well, I hope things stay quiet. I'd better get home before the little girls arrive." She smiled again and began heading for home, wishing she could have said something that would have left him laughing. Or nodding in agreement. Or anything that would have kept them talking for longer.

"Idiot," she murmured to herself once she was out of Tate's earshot. "He offered to pick you up—you should have jumped at the chance." But she didn't want anyone to get the wrong impression. She especially didn't want Tate to get the wrong impression. She didn't need an escort. She could manage her life just fine, despite her one mix-up with Allen.

Of course, it would be nice to develop a close friendship with him. Could a man and woman just be friends? She thought back to some of her coworkers at the hospital. They'd been friends, going for coffee together, sharing what was going on in their lives. No romantic entanglements there.

Still—she'd never felt that fluttery feeling around any of them that she did around Tate. And he still missed his wife. He was definitely not looking for involvement of a romantic nature. She had to remember that.

Not that she was, either. Maybe one day. Perhaps with a nice man who already had children, someone who would stick by her through thick and thin.

But it had been fun to do things with the sheriff on Saturday. Until her nice man came along, she and Tate could be friends.

Tate watched Faith walk away. He'd come to church late, not knowing if he'd find the time. Sitting in the back, he'd seen her in front of him, sitting with Janette. His parents were back early, which had surprised him. Once the service ended, they found him. His mother had fussed a bit over the bandage. The Kincaids had joined them and all teased him about the injury. Zack even hinted that it had its good aspects because Tate had met Faith as a result.

That sparked his mother's interest big-time. She'd begun suggesting he begin dating again about a year ago. Nothing too overt, but she worried about his being alone, she said. He believed the real reason was that she wanted grandchildren. She'd questioned Zack about Faith, and when others chimed in, she had a certain gleam in her eyes. Tate knew better than to touch that topic.

He returned to the patrol car. He and Mandy had talked about children, but had wanted to wait until they could afford to buy a house before starting a family. Now he had the house and no family in sight.

Since his return home, he'd become involved with some of the youth activities at the church, notably the basketball games in the summer. And the picnics and cakewalks and even some swim parties. He liked children. Who would have suspected?

As he pulled away from the curb, he wished he wasn't working today. He wished he could have gone with Jenny and her friends to see the puppies. While they played with them, he could have spent more time with Faith.

Nothing was going on around town, and he didn't like the way his thoughts kept returning to the pretty nurse. He'd head into the office and catch up on paperwork. That was guaranteed to keep his mind fully occupied.

"Thank You, God," Tate said aloud when he woke Wednesday morning to a steady drizzle. It was a gray and dreary day, the next-to-last Wednesday before Labor Day weekend, and after that the town returned to normal. The summer inhabitants would be gone until next May.

The rain gave him the excuse to pick up Faith for tonight's singles meeting. He'd seen her briefly at the clinic Monday when he had his stitches taken out. Once at the meeting, they'd be surrounded by others, focused on the rummage sale, on Bible study and on general conversation. No time to talk one-on-one. Driving her to and from the meeting would give them a little time together.

The day seemed to drag by. Once in the early afternoon, the sun peeked out. Tate tried to judge if the weather was turning, but was reassured some time later when the rain began again.

He called the clinic to remind Faith that he'd be picking her up shortly before seven. She was busy, so he left the message with Marjorie.

"I'll make sure she gets it," Marjorie said. "Nice of you to offer."

Did he hear a note of censure in her tone?

"Yeah, well, I'm going, so no sense in taking two cars."

"Oh, right. Conservation of gas and all. Amazing how everyone wants to help the new girl."

"Being neighborly," he said. He had heard something in her tone. What was that about?

When he arrived at her apartment that evening, Faith was watching for him. Before he could stop the car, she hurried down the steps, her umbrella keeping the drizzle off her face. He opened his door but she called, "Don't get wet, I can manage." She opened the passenger door, closed the umbrella and settled in. "Whew, it's not pouring, but it's so misty I think the air is saturated and the umbrella doesn't help a lot. Thanks for picking me up."

"Glad to do it." He headed for the church. "How're things going?"

"Fine on all fronts. You?"

"Quiet. We're gearing up for the big Labor Day weekend flings, then things should settle down until next summer."

"Umm, that's what Marjorie said. We've had a few tourists in with scrapes, cuts or bad sunburn. Most of the clinic's patients, however, are locals. I'm discussing with Dr. Mallory the idea of starting an expectant mothers class—what to expect, how to prepare— especially for first-time mothers."

"We don't already have something like that?" he asked.

"No. Women who want to breast-feed have had to go to Monkesville for La Leche classes. I want to com-

Get 2 Books FREE!

Love Inspired® Books,
a leading publisher of inspirational romance fiction, presents

Love Inspired

A series of contemporary love stories that will lift your spirits and reinforce important lessons about life, faith and love!

FREE BOOKS!
Get two free books by acclaimed, inspirational authors!

FREE GIFTS!
Get two exciting surprise gifts absolutely free!

Love Inspired

2 FREE BOOKS

▲ To get your 2 free books and 2 free gifts, affix this peel-off sticker to the reply card and mail it today!

We'd like to send you two free books to introduce you to the Love Inspired® series. Your two books have a combined cover price of $11.50 or more in the U.S. and $13.50 or more in Canada, but they are yours to keep absolutely FREE! We'll even send you two wonderful surprise gifts. You can't lose!

Love Inspired
Hannah's Daughters
Anna's Gift
Emma Miller

Love Inspired
5 YEARS
Seaside Reunion
Irene Hannon
Starfish Bay

Love Inspired
Big Sky Family
Charlotte Carter

Love Inspired
Building a Family
Lyn Cote
New Friends Street

Love Inspired
The Cowboy's Lady
CAROLYNE AARSEN
ROCKY MOUNTAIN HEIRS

Each of your **FREE** books is filled with jo faith and traditional values as men and women open their hearts to each oth and join together on a spiritual journey.

FREE BONUS GIFTS!

We'll send you two wonderful surprise gifts, worth about $10, absolutely FREE, just for giving Love Inspired books a try! Don't miss out—
MAIL THE REPLY CARD TODAY!

Visit us at
www.ReaderService.com

GET 2 FREE BOOKS!

HURRY!
Return this card today to get **2 FREE Books** and **2 FREE Bonus Gifts!**

Love Inspired.

YES! Please send me the 2 FREE Love Inspired® books and 2 free gifts for which I qualify. I understand that I am under no obligation to purchase anything further, as explained on the back of this card.

affix free books sticker here

❏ I prefer the regular-print edition
105/305 IDL FMRG

❏ I prefer the larger-print edition
122/322 IDL FMRG

Please Print

FIRST NAME

LAST NAME

ADDRESS

APT.#

CITY

STATE/PROV.

ZIP/POSTAL CODE

The Reader Service — Here's How it Works:

bine that with all the other aspects of pregnancy and delivery. Maybe even extend it to the first two or three months after a baby arrives. Lots of women have postpartum blues and don't realize that's normal. Anyway, that's what I've been doing while you're out keeping Rocky Point safe."

He laughed. "Not hard to do."

They parked near the entry to the fellowship hall and ran inside together. Their time for one-on-one was over for a couple of hours. Tate wished they could fast-forward the evening.

The meeting flew by, Faith thought as she and Tate got into his car a couple of hours later. They'd updated everyone on their team's rummage-sale donation pledges, spent time in small groups studying a portion of Second Timothy. Then just socialized with the cake and coffee some of the women had prepared.

"I can't believe how much stuff will be at the rummage sale," she said, still amazed at the quantity of donations each team had promised to deliver.

He drove down Main Street. "We'll have the entire fellowship hall filled with tables piled high with items. Clothing in one area, appliances and other small items in another. Furniture and lawn tools are put around the perimeter. For two days, Friday and Saturday, it's bedlam. Then cleaned up Saturday night so the hall can be used Sunday."

"Marylou was right—it's a lot of work. It's going to be fun, though."

"It is. My mother always works the sale. She says that, once a year, she knows she'll get to see everyone in town."

"So your parents are home," she said. "I thought

I might have seen them on Sunday. How did your mother take your bump on the head?"

"Fussed just as I knew she would. I was counting on getting the stitches out before she saw. But they came home late Saturday evening."

When he reached her apartment, she gathered her things. "You don't need to get out. I'll dash up the steps and be inside in no time."

"I don't mind." Tate got out and opened the door for her. Then he followed her up the steps.

She hesitated at the door. "Do you want to come in? To see the puppies? They're really growing."

He hesitated a moment, then shook his head. "Not tonight. Maybe next time."

"Good night, Tate," she said, feeling both relieved and disappointed that he hadn't stayed.

She waited until he left before taking Maggie out for one last visit to the grassy spot she favored. Back inside, Faith dried her hair, got into her pajamas and curled up with the Bible, reviewing the passage they'd studied that evening. "Lord, I feel Your presence here more than ever before. Am I in Your sights? Please, let me know what You expect from me so I can do Your will. Thanks for the new friends. I'm glad I came here. Amen."

But it was one friend whose face danced in her mind above all the others—Tate Johnson.

Jenny Kincaid and her friends were becoming regular visitors at Faith's apartment. The three girls loved the puppies and all had prevailed upon their parents to let them adopt one when the puppies were old enough. They spent their visits on the floor in the kitchen, tumbling around with the puppies, laughing and shrieking in delight. Through those frequent visits, Faith met each of the parents, and spent a lot of time with the girls. Names were discussed, puppies earmarked for each girl. She felt a bit sad to think that one day all the puppies would be gone, but at least they'd be nearby and Faith made each girl promise to let her see them from time to time.

"You should consider obedience training," she told them at their Thursday afternoon visit. "That way they'll be nicely behaved and you can take them anywhere that allows dogs."

"How do we do that?" Melissa asked.

"I'll find out. I might take Maggie. She has nice manners, except for pulling on the leash. I want to make sure I also know how to be a good owner."

"We could all take training together," Jenny said, bubbling over with excitement. "That way we could help each other and the dogs would know each other."

"That we could. I don't know how old puppies have to be for obedience training. Maggie's sure old enough," Faith said, touched that the little girl wanted to spend time with her. She wasn't used to children, but found these three easy to be with. Of course, most of their attention focused on the puppies.

That evening Faith called Tate. If anyone in town knew about obedience-training classes, he would.

He didn't answer, so she left a brief message on his machine.

Between patients the next morning, Marjorie came into the exam room Faith was straightening.

"You got a call from the sheriff a while back. He said you called him. I know you're making a play for the man, but the least you could do is keep your private life out of the clinic. Personal calls are not encouraged."

Faith stared at her in shock. "I'm not making a play for him," she said, astonished that Marjorie would even think such a thing.

"Oh, come on, you're doing all you can to attract his attention. Hugging him right in front of everyone in the reception area. Now calling and leaving messages on his phone. You may have fooled some of the people in town, but not me," she scoffed. "Tate Johnson's one of the finest men around. He suffered a horrible loss when his wife died. If he were looking to get married again, I'm sure he has no need to take up with some stranger. There are a lot of nice girls who were born and raised right here in Rocky Point."

Faith couldn't believe her ears. "Marjorie, you don't have a clue what you're talking about. He's been helpful in finding the owner of the dog." And in introducing her around at the singles group. She knew better than Marjorie that Tate was not looking for involvement at this time.

"I have eyes. Anyway, I've delivered the message." With a frown, she turned and left the room.

Faith shook her head in disbelief. Marjorie was definitely not in the new-friend category, but Faith couldn't believe how nasty she sounded. And the way she spoke, Faith had no illusions about how she felt about Faith and Tate's friendship. Was it a personal dislike, or was Marjorie equally distrustful of all newcomers to town?

"Lord, help me here," she prayed softly. "I don't know how to get on Marjorie's good side. Show me the way to get through to her."

She almost overlooked that Tate had returned her

call. She hoped she hadn't sounded like it was an emergency that he needed to call from work.

Faith went home for lunch. After Maggie had a brief run, Faith called the sheriff's office.

"Hi," Tate said when her call was put through.

"Hi. I didn't mean to make my message sound urgent," she began.

"It didn't. Oh, because I called you at the clinic?"

"Marjorie said we need to keep personal business separate," she said, still stinging from the woman's attitude.

"As if Doc Mallory would care. Anyway, what's up?"

"I'm thinking of taking Maggie to an obedience-training class and wanted to know if there were any around. I thought you might know."

"Only one I've heard of is over in Monkesville."

"Umm. I suggested the girls might take the puppies when they get older. But that's going to be hard if it's clear over there."

"If everyone goes at once, one parent or another can drive."

"Right, three girls and three puppies all in one car?" She could imagine the bedlam that would produce.

"Good point," he said. "Find out if the trainer would come here if the class is big enough. Maybe there're other people in town who would sign up."

"That's a great idea."

"So aside from the no-no phone call, how's your day going?"

She was not going to bring up the difficulties she had with the receptionist. "Pretty good. How about yours?"

"Same old, same old."

Conscious of the comments of the older woman that morning, Faith didn't want to talk too long. She never wanted Tate to think she was making a play for him.

"Well, thanks for the info. I'll check it out and see what the trainer says. Hope the rest of your day is good."

She walked back through town to the clinic, noticing Rachel out in front of her antiques store sweeping the sidewalk. A glazier had replaced the broken window earlier in the week.

"Hi, Rachel. I saw you were able to repair the damage quickly."

"Hi, Faith." The storekeeper smiled warmly. "Yes, Tate made sure the man responsible forked over the money to fix it before he left jail. And with Tate's father's connections, he put me in touch with Mr. Abrams, who came right out. The sign painter's coming next week and it'll all look the way it used to. Tell him thanks for me, will you?"

"You'll probably see him before I do," Faith said, taken aback.

"I doubt it. If so, I'll say it first. I'm still watching out for that table you want."

"Thanks." Faith nodded and moved on, wondering if Marjorie was right and people thought she was trying to attract the attentions of the sheriff.

She sure hoped that wasn't the case, but she couldn't get Marjorie's insinuations out of her head for the rest of the afternoon.

Stopping at the grocery store on the way home from work, Faith recognized a couple of the other shoppers and greeted them by name. Mrs. Bradshaw was there and stopped beside Faith. "Tell the doctor that the latest medicines are working real well." She flexed her fingers. "No pain at all. Finally."

Faith smiled. "I'll do that. I'm glad that's helping you."

Mrs. Bradshaw looked at the things in Faith's cart. "A young man needs more than that. A nice pot roast would be wonderful. My Fred always liked pot roast."

"I have no young man," Faith said, already knowing where this was going.

"Well, if you want to keep it a secret, you shouldn't be hugging him in front of everyone. I still say a pot roast will make him sit up and take notice."

Faith smiled, anxious to escape. "Thanks, Mrs. Bradshaw. I'll keep that in mind."

"The sheriff's a good man, coming home to help his parents, saving that child the way he did. No one finer in town."

Faith nodded. "We're just friends," she said.

Mrs. Bradshaw smiled broadly. "Well, of course. You two have a nice dinner." She pushed her cart down the aisle while Faith wondered how she could correct the mistaken impression.

Maybe ignoring it would work best.

Once dinner was over and the dog walked, Faith picked up the mystery she'd been trying to finish for two weeks and stretched out on the sofa. The story wasn't as compelling as it once had been. Her thoughts kept drifting to Tate, wondering what he was doing and if anyone had even hinted to him that there was something going on between them.

She should go to the singles meeting next week on her own.

But if he asked to accompany her, could she refuse?

* * *

Tate pulled into his parents' driveway Friday evening. His mother had invited him to dinner and he never passed up the chance to sample her cooking. He hadn't spent much time with them since they returned from their trip and he wanted to hear all about it.

"Hey, Tate, good to see you, son," his father greeted him when he entered the house. Sitting in front of the television, with a sports report going full blast, Todd Johnson waved and muted the sound.

"Hi, Dad. You're looking rested." Tate took in the scene as his father rose to give him a hug.

"I am. We were on the go the entire time in Boston, but a different kind of activity from home, so I feel fit as a fiddle."

"Where's Mom?" Tate asked.

"In the kitchen—where else? That woman does love to cook," he said affectionately. "She gave me a rundown on every meal we had in Boston, telling me what spices were used, how she would have prepared it. Honestly, I think she should have started her own restaurant."

"I'll go say hi. Be back in a few."

Tate continued through to the kitchen where he found his mother stirring something on the stove. The aromas made his mouth water.

"Hi, Mom."

"Oh, Tate, there you are. Nice of you to come see us when I know you must have had other plans." She gave him a quick hug. "Want something to drink?"

"I'll get a soda. No other plans."

"Oh, well, that's too bad." She looked thoughtful for a moment. "You could have brought Faith to dinner."

Tate raised an eyebrow at that. "Why would I do

that?" He was not up to his mother's matchmaking this evening. Bill Raymond had made some comment this afternoon about Tate seeing the new nurse in town when he'd run into Bill outside the post office.

"Well, so we'd get to know her and all," Cecile Johnson said.

"She attends Trinity. You can see her Sunday," he said, popping open the soda and taking a drink. "Can I help?"

"No, I have everything under control. Dinner'll be ready in twenty minutes.'

"I'll keep Dad company, then," he said. Walking down the hall, he wondered why all of a sudden people thought he was seeing Faith.

He was, but not like that. She was new in town. He was just showing her the ropes. They weren't dating. He didn't date. He had loved his wife and still mourned her death.

And Faith was nothing like Mandy.

"Mom chase you out?" his father asked when he returned to the living room.

"She says she doesn't need any help." He wondered where she'd gotten the idea that he was interested in Faith. He'd been very clear with the new nurse that he was not looking for romance. She'd been burned herself. She was not looking for any involvement, either. Which made their friendship perfect.

And that's all it was—a friendship. He'd never even touched her.

Well, except for the hug she'd given him at the clinic. But that had been in gratitude for finding out she could keep the dog. And a couple of times when their hands had brushed against each other while they were passing puppies around.

He looked at his father who had started watching TV again. What did he think? And why had Bill Raymond made that comment?

In less than fifteen minutes his mom called them to dinner.

"Tell me about your trip," Tate said after they had said grace over the evening meal and began to put food on the plates.

"It was fabulous," his mother said. "We saw all the historic sites, like the old North Church and Bunker Hill. Then Old Ironsides."

"Hadn't you seen all that before? You took me when I was a kid."

"But that's been years. And when we visited you and Mandy, we mostly came to see you two. It was fun to play tourist again. And the food was marvelous. Better than a cruise ship," his father said.

Tate laughed. "When were you on a cruise ship?

"I know about them. Just never wanted to go."

"Sure. So what did you like the most?" Tate couldn't wait to hear what his father's take on their sightseeing was.

"The waterfront," his dad said quickly.

"I liked the shopping," his mother added. "You should see the pretty dress I bought to wear to the wedding. I was going to wear my old blue one, but I really liked this one. So are plans well under way?"

"Far as I know. We have the rehearsal scheduled for Friday, then the ceremony on Saturday, reception afterward. I'll be glad when it's over."

"Oh, I love weddings," his mom said with a big smile. "Yours was so lovely. I hope this one for Joe works out better than his first one."

Tate nodded. "I think it will."

His mother looked at him speculatively. "So how did you meet Faith?"

"The nurse?" He tried to downplay the entire situation. "When Jesse's boat rammed into my head. She's the new nurse at the clinic and assisted the doctor."

"Yes, you've said that. But you've seen her away from the clinic, so I've been hearing," his mother persisted.

"A couple of times. I took her to the singles group at church, just to introduce her around." Tate tried to sound casual about it. Who was gossiping to his mother? One of the drawbacks of living in a small town where so many people knew him.

"That was nice of you," his mother said. "Honey, do you want some more green beans?" she asked her husband.

Tate waited for more questions, but after his father took the bowl of beans, his mother began to tell him more about their vacation. Tate was glad for the change of subject.

"So, next weekend we're planning our summer barbecue. Do you think you'll have Saturday afternoon off?" his mother asked as she was preparing to clear the table when the meal finished.

"I don't know, Mom. It's the last weekend before Labor Day and usually I ask for the entire crew to be on duty. Hard to take off when everyone else is working."

"We go through this each year," she sighed.

He smiled at her indulgently. "Why not have the barbecue later, then?" he asked.

"The weather could change. It just works out best now. The church picnic's on Labor Day, so folks have that to go to. Later in the year isn't the same. Plus, this year the weekend after Labor Day is the wedding."

"Are you two going to the church picnic?" Trinity had its annual end-of-summer picnic at Carlisle Beach on Labor Day each year.

"I don't know.... I expect we'll stop in for a while. But it's more for families, don't you think? Remember what fun we all had when you and Stacy were younger?" his mother reflected with a fond smile. "Couldn't get you kids out of the water sometimes."

He and his sister had loved those picnics.

"We're a family," Tate said.

"I meant with younger children. We loved going when you and your sister were little."

"We were younger then," his dad added. "Didn't mind the sand as much."

Tate laughed. His father always complained about the sand getting in the car and then into the house. "Yeah, but if you don't go, sand will still find its way."

"You going?" his dad asked.

"Only if there's trouble."

His mother looked at him and smiled. "Then let's see if you can make it to our gathering. I'm asking the Brewers, the Ballards, the Kincaids, the Winters and the Pollards, of course. I haven't seen much of Zack since he's been back." She took a breath. "And I want to see Bill Winter. I heard he's back at work a couple of days a week. Amazing to think he had a kidney transplant only a month ago."

Tate nodded. Marcie's dad had come through a kidney transplant and regained his former health with remarkable speed. The annual summer barbecue was a family tradition going back to when he and his sister were kids. He'd do his best to arrange a few hours off to attend.

If he didn't fear that his mother would read more into it than warranted, he'd suggest she invite Faith. It would be a good place for her to get to know people better. She already saw Gillian a few times a week when Jenny went to see the puppies. She didn't know Marcie as well, or Ally Ballard. She'd fit right in.

But with the earlier comments ringing in his ears, he wasn't going there at all.

As he drove home later, Tate went through town. It was out of his direct route to his house, but he wanted to make sure things were okay. When he drove by the waterfront, he glanced up at the window of Faith's apartment. It was dark. Was she out? He wondered where she could be. Maybe she'd just gone to bed early.

The thought of another man taking her on a date wouldn't dissipate as he reached home. Not that he'd begrudge her that. But who in town would be suitable? He couldn't think of anyone.

When Faith returned home Saturday from her shift at the clinic, her new answering machine was flashing. Had a friend from Portland called? She'd given her cell number to her closest friends, who called periodically. But who had her home phone?

She pressed the replay button and was surprised to hear an unknown female voice.

"Faith Stewart? This is Cecile Johnson. Tate's mother. We're having our summer barbecue next Saturday and wanted to include you. I know we haven't met yet, but any friend of Tate's is more than welcome.

I think you'll know several of the other guests. The Kincaids will be here. And Tate, of course, if he can get off work. Do plan to join us. Come around three. We'll visit, have dinner and just enjoy ourselves."

She ended the call with her phone number.

Faith played it again. Tate's mother was definitely inviting her to what seemed to be a family tradition— a summer barbecue.

"Well, Maggie, now what do we do? Go and start the rumor mill humming? Or stay and miss a great opportunity to learn more about the sheriff and cement friendships with others in town?"

She sat down on the floor and played with the puppies while discussing the matter with the mama dog.

"I fended off an inquiry at the store the other day. Today Marjorie was snippy again. I understand her being miffed that I took the job she hoped her niece would get." But did her niece hope for a friendship with the sheriff, too?

Maggie wagged her tail and tried to lick Faith. Her laughter rang out as she fended off the dog.

She wanted to ask Tate about the event, but hesitated because she was overly conscious of Marjorie's scathing comments about calling the sheriff and making a pest of herself. Maybe she'd see him at church in the morning and could ask him then. He'd be polite, of course, but maybe he'd rather she not join them. He wouldn't want to give rise to talk of an incipient romance any more than she did.

Why did people have to gossip?

Faith still had not decided what to do when she arrived at church the next morning. The day was a bit blustery. Rain was expected later in the week, to the dismay of the vacationers. Not many visitors at the church, but Faith had heard some bemoaning the end of summer yesterday as she'd walked home, passing them on the sidewalk.

She greeted everyone with a smile. Those she already knew, she stopped to chat with for a minute. Stan, from the singles group, asked her to join them for lunch at Marcie's. "I'd love to. I'll meet everyone there," she said, glad to have plans. Pleased with the easygoing friendships she was making.

She saw the Johnsons as she entered. She recognized them from the previous week. She should have called back to answer the invitation. Looking for Tate, she didn't see him. She really wanted to talk to him before accepting—or declining.

"Tate working this morning?" one of the women from the singles group asked when she saw Faith.

"I expect so," she said. This was getting out of hand. She didn't know Tate's plans any more than Janette or Stan did.

"He'll come if he can," another said, with a smile at Faith.

Was she reading into things that weren't there? Or was there a knowing look in the woman's expression? Surely members of the singles group knew better than others that everyone was there for friendship, not to start a romantic relationship.

Faith sat with Janette again, moving in enough to leave space for anyone who came later. When the music started, she was startled to see Tate walking in. He slipped into the pew next to her, wearing his uniform without the utility belt.

"I'm taking downtime for this. Still on call, so I hope the phone doesn't go off," he whispered as she moved over to give him more room.

Janette leaned in front of Faith to smile a welcome. "Tell him about lunch," she whispered to Faith.

"A bunch of us from the singles group are meeting at Marcie's for lunch," Faith murmured, leaning close enough to smell his aftershave. It started her heart racing. She gripped the hymnal tightly, her eyes meeting his. For a second it was as if they were the only two people there. His dark eyes were warm, and his smile had her heart tripping again with that dimple showing.

Then the organ music started and everyone rose to sing the opening hymn. Faith flipped open her book to the page and began singing. She was startled when Tate reached out to hold the hymnal with her and began to sing. His deep voice was lovely. She felt an uplifting in her heart to praise the Lord in song beside Tate.

It was more difficult this time to focus on what the pastor was saying with Tate sitting just inches away. She was conscious of the invitation that his mother had given. Did he know? She wished she could have asked him before the service began, just to have it settled.

Finally concentrating on the pastor's message she listened to the lesson from Paul about faith unceasing. That's what she needed, never any doubts about her future, just enduring faith.

A peace descended and she was refreshed by the sermon.

Tate listened to the words Pastor John spoke and wondered why it was hard for men to have that rock-solid faith. He'd studied the Bible over the years and knew the promise of the Lord. But when bad things happened—like Mandy's death—his own faith wobbled. He had prayed and come to peace with the situation. But Paul would have soldiered on without the wavering faith. He wanted that same kind of steadfast spirituality.

When the service ended, he rose and stepped in the aisle, waiting for Faith and Janette to proceed him out. On the front steps he replaced his hat carefully. The area that had healed was still a bit tender.

"So, can you take time to join us for lunch?" Janette asked.

Tate looked down at her. "I'll check in and let you know," he said.

"Tate, there you are," his mother came down the shallow steps and hurried over to him.

"I didn't see you in church."

"I came in just as the service started," he said, giving her a hug.

She smiled at the two women. "Ah, Faith Stewart, just the young woman I wanted to see."

"Hello, Mrs. Johnson," Faith said, knowing what was coming. She glanced at Janette, wondering what she thought about all this.

"I'm pleased to meet you at last," Cecile Johnson said with a friendly smile.

"Sorry, Mom, I thought you already had met. You remember Janette, of course."

"Of course I do. How are you?"

"Doing fine, Cecile. A group of us are heading for lunch at Marcie's. I'll see you there, Faith," Janette said as she turned and went to catch up with another member of their group.

"I didn't hear from you, so thought I'd catch you today to see if you're coming next week," Cecile Johnson said.

"I got your message, but I didn't have a chance to respond," Faith replied.

Tate looked back and forth between the women. Faith looked at him with silent entreaty. What was going on? His mother had invited Faith to the barbecue?

"Well, we do hope you can make it. My husband cooks the best barbecue ribs in town!"

He looked at his mother. Why had she invited Faith without even mentioning it to him?

"Tell her, Tate, how much fun it is," his mother said, seemingly oblivious to the rising tension.

"It's fun." He wasn't sure how he felt. One thing for sure—he and his mother needed to have a chat. Was she matchmaking? After what Faith had gone through before with the fiancé who didn't stick around, he didn't want her to be the center of speculation.

"I'll have to let you know, if I can wait a bit longer," Faith said. "I work at the clinic Saturdays."

"I know it's open until one. We don't start until around three and go on until after dark. We'll have a lot of people for you to meet and some you already know, like the Kincaids." She gave Faith a warm smile. "Lots of kids, actually, as most of Tate's friends who come have children already. I can't wait until we have our own grandchildren…"

Tate wanted to groan. Definitely matchmaking. And she hadn't a clue about the true situation with Faith. Every so often, his mother let something slip about wanting grandchildren. Let his sister provide them. Were they after her as much to get married and have kids? He'd have to ask her the next time they talked. She lived in New York and came home to Rocky Point only on rare occasions.

"We have to go, Mom," he said, taking control before anything worse came from his mother.

He took Faith's arm and walked across the lawn to the sidewalk.

"Sorry about that," he said. "If you don't want to go, just say no."

"I'd hoped to find you before I had to answer to see what you thought. I mean, it's really nice of your mother to include me, but is there a hidden message there?"

"Like she's matchmaking? My guess is yes," he said.

"Then I should stay away."

"The barbecue is fun. You'd know some of the other guests. The Kincaids always come, and Marylou and Sam. I also think Ally Ballard would be someone you'd like. And there are the kids. I believe this year Sean and his mother are coming."

"Who's Sean?"

"Oh, I forgot, you probably haven't met him. He's one of the teens in Zack's driving club."

"Zack has a driving club?" Faith had never heard of a driving club.

"Do you know who he is?"

"Joe's brother," she said.

"He's also a grand prix racer who has won a ton of races in Europe. Sean was a kid who didn't have a lot of direction or male influence when Zack sort of took him under his wing. We found a place for a driving track and now a bunch of the teens from church belong to this club, where they practice driving techniques and hang out together."

"And Sean is one of them?"

He nodded. "The first. He's all right. Picked him up

once for underage drinking, but we got that straightened out. He's doing great, thanks to Zack."

"And what part do you play?" Faith asked, fascinated to learn another facet of Tate's life.

"Not much. I meet with them from time to time. Let them go on ride-alongs when I expect it to be perfectly safe."

"And play basketball," she guessed.

"That, too. Want to come to the game Tuesday?"

She raised a brow. "Are you playing?"

"I'm 100 percent fit, so yeah, I'll probably be playing."

"Maybe." It would be fun to see him play and watch him interact with the kids from church. Though, maybe she shouldn't…

"I'm not going if it's going to give rise to speculation that we are seeing each other," she said, glancing around, already conscious of their talking together in front of the church. Would this fuel speculation?

Tate should have rejoiced that she felt the same way he did. But instead, he felt a twinge of disappointment. "Would that be so bad?" he asked.

"I don't want to mislead anyone." Her tone held exasperation.

"We know the truth and that's all that's important. Think of it as giving yourself a chance to get to know your neighbors better. Once the bad weather comes, everyone tends to stay inside and there are a few activities around town. Lots of people come to the games, not just parents."

"If you're sure."

He reached out to touch her shoulder, wishing he could go to lunch with her, spend the afternoon together. Even if it would give rise to the speculation they wanted to avoid. A couple more weeks and he'd be back to weekends free. Then maybe they could do some things together.

"I'm sure. I'd offer to pick you up, but—"

"No, I'll get there myself. I know where the high school is. What about the barbecue?"

"Come. You'll have a good time."

Faith considered it for a moment. She really wanted to go. "Okay. It's on your head if gossip runs rampant. Tell me where your parents live."

He gave her directions and then reluctantly said, "I'm going back to work. You enjoy lunch."

"Thanks. See ya."

He watched her walk away, before turning to head for the patrol car he'd left in the church parking lot. She was still too thin. But her color was good. Her skin was like peaches and cream. He knew now where that saying came from—women like Faith. She looked nothing like Mandy, but he was discovering a fondness for curly blond hair and a sun-kissed complexion.

Whoa, he thought, no point going down that road. He'd had his shot at love. It hadn't come with guarantees.

Unceasing faith echoed in his head. Was that a message directed toward him? He wondered if the Lord planned to touch his heart a second time with a love that could lead to marriage and a shared life.

But was he strong enough to risk falling in love, knowing it might not last a lifetime?

Chapter Six

Tate made sure his drive through the town later that afternoon coincided with the time Faith usually walked Maggie. The sidewalks were crowded with tourists, some returning for a day on the water, others out for an early stroll. The ice-cream parlor was doing a booming business, as evidenced by those walking along window-shopping while licking cones.

He parked near the marina and got out. Paperwork and several sweeps of the town had occupied his day. It felt good to be on the grass, taking in the sea air. A moment later, he caught sight of Faith walking with Maggie. The dog bounded along, to the end of her leash, then dashed back to Faith, danced around her legs, then lurched forward again.

She was laughing. Tate watched her, knowing she hadn't seen him yet. He smiled at the sound of her laughter. It was infectious.

Maggie saw him and barked, running directly to him, pulling Faith along. Her laughter rang out again.

"Goodness, she recognized you!" she exclaimed when she was close enough.

"Hey, girl," Tate said, leaning over to pet the dog. "Out for a bit of freedom from the kids?"

"I think you're right. She puts up with them for only so long, then jumps the barrier and stretches out in the living room." She sighed. "They're a handful now. Running around, skidding on the linoleum. You'll have to come see them."

"Maybe when I get off duty this evening. Around seven?" he said casually, still petting the dog.

"Sure, that'd be perfect." Faith looked around, then back at Tate as he rose.

"Want to sit on a bench?" he asked.

"For a few minutes. We need all the exercise we can get while we're out, you know," she said, walking over and sitting while Maggie began sniffing every blade of grass within reach.

"This is nice," she murmured. "In Portland, I was so caught up in work and things, I didn't go out just to be outdoors. I was always going from one place to another. Maggie gets me out and I like it," she said.

"Nice time of year, too. September'll be good, though the nights will begin to cool off. But with most of the tourists gone, the town settles down. You'll see a difference, one I hope you like. It can get pretty quiet."

"I'm not exactly a party girl," she said, watching the dog. "Do you get bored in the winter—I mean, after Boston, this has to be pretty tame."

"Not bored. I have plenty to do with the house. And there's enough going on to satisfy me. If I want to do something special, I can always visit." He glanced her way. "I'm thinking of going to New York in the fall. Maybe stay with my sister for a week or so."

"Umm, that sounds nice. I went there once—it

was amazing. Lots to see, so many different neighborhoods. I didn't begin to see it all," she said.

"What did you like best?"

"The food and the shopping," she replied without hesitation.

"I'm not much on shopping, but I like to eat."

She laughed. Tate was struck again with how much he liked hearing her laugh. Her eyes sparkled. The sound was sweet. He liked knowing that she had come back from adversity and illness to be the vibrant, healthy woman he now saw.

"So, want me to pick you up for the singles meeting this week, rain or shine?" he asked.

She looked at him, then caught her lip between her teeth and looked away. "I'm not sure," she said. Throwing him a glance, she shrugged. "I think some people are pairing us up. I've had more than one person suggest that I talk to you about something, as if I have better access to you than they do."

Tate reached out and took her free hand in his, liking the touch of her skin, the warm softness. "Hey, let people talk. We know we're friends."

She took a breath and looked at him. "We *are* friends. I cherish that. But you're very special and I'm afraid if we spend a lot of time together, gossip will get out of hand. And neither of us wants that."

"No, but we can't live our lives based on other people's gossip," he said, suddenly worried that she was going to suggest they stop seeing each other. "Neither of us wants the complications of a romantic relationship, right?" he asked, wanting that reaffirmed.

"Not the complications, but I did like being part of a couple. I thought I had found a man to build a life with. I liked that. You're much more than Allen can ever hope to be." She looked away for a moment. Then took a deep breath. "What if I fall for you?"

Tate watched her as she stared at the water. That took guts to say. "Why not see where being together leads us?" He raised her hand and kissed the back of her fingers. "Unceasing faith—wasn't that today's message? If we both have that, we'll go where the Lord leads. Together or not, He'll show us the way."

She gazed into his eyes and Tate saw the confusion in hers. Then she smiled. "I need to practice that unceasing-faith part. I know the Lord has me in His hands. He brought me through the cancer and I didn't die of a broken heart, either. So I'll do my part," she said softly. "But no romance for a while. Let's just see what happens as friends."

"No romance." The minute he said the words, he wanted to take them back. He wanted to kiss her, bring her flowers and watch her smile. Spend evenings with her when work was over and they could spend the time together without interruption.

He'd honor the promise. "For now," he added.

"Okay, for now." She rose and tugged gently until he released her hand.

"I need to get Mama Dog home to the kids. See you around seven."

Tate sat a little longer on the bench, wondering when he'd opened his heart to the possibility of change. When he first lost his wife, he'd vowed he'd never put himself at risk for heartbreak again. Yet, now he was chafing at the restriction of no romance with a woman he'd only met a couple of weeks ago.

He wasn't in love with Faith. But if love came, would he turn from it? Could he be strong enough to risk his heart a second time?

He rose. He wasn't going anywhere and it seemed as if Faith was settling in and would be around for the long haul. Time enough to see what the Lord had in store. He glanced at his watch. Only a little over ninety minutes until he'd see her again. He wanted to go home and change when his shift ended. Tonight he was not the sheriff. Just a friend visiting a friend.

Faith was smiling when she entered the clinic the next morning. The evening with Tate had been fun. They'd made popcorn and watched an old movie on TV. Talking during the commercials, watching the show and commenting on scenes that seemed a bit over the top had been fun. He had gone out with her and Maggie for their evening walk. They had strolled to the marina park, which she was starting to think of as their place.

Which wasn't so wise.

He'd left after the walk, citing work the next morning. She thought he'd been going to kiss her, but he'd paused a moment near the bottom of the steps and then wished her good-night.

Faith was a little disappointed, yet hadn't she said no romance? Even if he had wanted to kiss her, he was too much of a gentleman to go against her wishes.

Now she wished she'd kept her mouth shut!

She agreed to attend the singles meeting with him. Before that was the basketball game. And there was next weekend's barbecue to look forward to.

"We have a busy schedule today—I hope you're ready to work," Marjorie greeted her a moment later. The older woman looked more cross than usual and Faith sighed softly.

Lord, please help me find a way to work with her in harmony...

The day was hectic, with two emergencies in the morning and a full load of kids getting final checkups and shots before school started. The teenagers the doctor saw needed forms filled out for athletics. The younger kids needed booster shots. They were running behind schedule from ten o'clock on, so Faith had a short lunch and left the clinic almost forty minutes after closing.

She took Maggie for a walk and then put on old clothes, fixed dinner and checked the mail. The reminder notice for her semiannual checkup had come. She rarely got any mail except bills and junk mail. Her friends from Portland called, rather than wrote. She saw people in Rocky Point almost on a daily basis.

Next Wednesday. She checked her calendar and saw that she had it down. Had she asked Dr. Mallory for the afternoon off? She'd better double-check. She knew she'd mentioned it at her initial interview, but he might not have noted it.

She finished the mystery book right before going to sleep. She wondered if Tate read mysteries or would find too much fabrication about the way the sheriff's department ran things to enjoy them. The few mysteries that she'd read that centered around a hospital had so many errors they annoyed her no end.

It rained again on Tuesday, but she and Maggie braved the elements long enough for the dog to take care of business. Then Faith headed for the high-school gym.

There were more people on hand than she expected. Faith parked close to the gym, so she didn't get too wet running inside. She looked around. Bleachers had been extended on both sides of the court and were already filling up. She tried to see if it mattered which side she sat on, but both sides had room and were about equally filled. She crossed to sit on the far side, walking up and then smiling as she sat in an empty space about halfway up. Those already seated scooted over to make more room.

Boys were practicing their throws. A line of players sat on the lowest bench, watching the others and listening to a man who was probably the coach. It was noisy and festive.

Then a referee blew his whistle long and loud. Silence descended. Everyone looked at him as he took a mike from his back pocket.

"Good evening, everyone. We're back."

Everyone laughed. Excitement seemed to fill the air.

"Team A from Trinity consists of Brian, Mark, AJ, Thom and Seth. Team B starters are Peter, Tate, Jerry, Phil and Scooter. May the best team win!"

The game was fast and Faith soon was caught up in cheering them all on. Both teams had two men and three boys, with others on the sidelines. Team A wore blue jerseys and Team B wore red. She spotted Tate as soon as the game began. He moved out onto the court, taller than the others on his team. That had to be good. As the game progressed, it seemed as if everyone rotated in and out in some random fashion.

When he took the floor a second time, her cheers became louder. First Team A was ahead, then Team B. As the first half ended, the two were still close in score, with Tate's Team B in the lead by two points.

"Great game, huh?" the woman next to her said,

her eyes still on the players now milling around at the center of the court.

"Yes," Faith agreed, straining to see if she could spot Tate.

"It's a short halftime, not worth fighting the crowd to go get refreshments," the woman said.

Faith nodded, then saw Tate at the same moment he was scanning the crowd. For her?

When he seemed to be looking her way, she waved. He smiled and waved back.

"Friend of yours?" the woman asked.

"Yes."

"Nice of the men to rally with the boys," she said. "I'm Erma Decker. My grandson is playing on Team A. Who're you rooting for?"

"I'm Faith Stewart and my friend is Tate Johnson. He's on Team B."

The woman leaned toward her. "I don't go to Trinity—we live in Monkesville. But I recognize the players week after week. This is a fun outing for us." She tapped her husband on the shoulder and he turned to her, interrupting his chat with his neighbor.

"Meet Faith, Aaron. She has a player on Team B."

"Pleasure," Aaron said with a grin, then turned back to his neighbor.

"This is my first game," Faith confided.

"Oh, they're so much fun. Rocky Point's sheriff started them, thought the kids needed an outlet in summer. He's got some smart ideas, I say."

"That's the sheriff I waved to," Faith said, startled to learn that this activity had been Tate's idea.

"Nice-looking young man," Erma said, smiling down at Tate and waving. "I didn't know he was the sheriff. I like that—practice what he preaches."

"The entire Trinity congregation seems really involved with the kids in the church."

"Good…gives them values and standards. Oh, the halftime is over. See, not worth the effort to fight the crowd. Sorry I can't root for your team. Have to support my grandson's, right?"

"Right." The second half went even faster. Faith and Erma exchanged comments when plays were good or missed. Neither seemed that concerned about winning. Faith was just as likely to cheer on a Team A player who was going for a basket as she was Tate's team.

When the game ended, Team A had won by a mere four points. Each Team B member congratulated the winners in the midst of the cheering from all fans.

Faith walked down the bleachers slowly, looking for Tate. He waited at the bottom and reached out for her when she got to the floor, pulling her away from the crowd now heading for the exit.

"You came," he said. "How'd you like it?"

"That was great. I heard this whole thing was your idea. Fabulous. The kids and guys all seemed to be having fun." When she was jostled by someone behind her, Tate reached out to steady her.

"Just an idea that took off. Glad to hear that you enjoyed yourself."

"Hey, great game, Sheriff," a fan called.

"Sorry your team didn't win," Faith said, moving so she wasn't bumped by another couple rushing by.

"Team B won last week. Sometimes we do, sometimes we don't. Everyone's a winner, however, just from the fun and activity."

"Nice shot you made from center court." A man stopped to slap Tate on the back. He grinned at Faith and moved on.

Tate nodded, smiled at some other people and looked back at Faith.

"Keeps kids out of trouble, right?" she said.

"Some of them. Wait while I shower and I'll drive you home."

She shook her head. "Actually, it was pouring rain when I came, so I drove. Besides, it's getting late. I'll see you tomorrow at the singles group."

"Hey, Tate, you're feeling better, I see," one of the men from the church said. "Great game. Next time put Harold in earlier. He's a sleeper."

"Will do. Thanks." He looked at Faith. "I'll swing by and pick you up tomorrow," he said.

"If it's nice, I want to walk."

"Sounds like a plan. I'll swing by and walk with you."

Another couple came up to talk to him, and Faith smiled and left, already looking forward to Wednesday. She hoped the weather would clear. A stroll through town to and from the church in the evening would allow more time with Tate.

The next morning Faith was counting the hours until she saw Tate again when she knocked on the exam room door and opened it slightly to find an irate patient.

"I have been waiting more than forty minutes. This is outrageous, and I'm going to tell the doctor," Muriel Foster said. "I have never had to wait this long. Was there an emergency? The least you could have done was told me. Then I could have decided whether or not to wait."

Faith was taken aback. She double-checked the folder and saw the time noted when the woman had arrived, almost forty-five minutes ago. But the flag by the door had not been flipped, denoting a patient waiting, until a moment or two ago. She would have noticed.

"I'm so sorry. I didn't know you were here," Faith said. "I'll let the doctor know you're ready and have been kept waiting. He won't be long."

"Well, I never! I have better things to do than sit around here all morning. How can you say you didn't know I was here?" she huffed. "Marjorie sent me back. She knew I was here. I'm not even sick—just in for a checkup."

"I apologize, Mrs. Foster. I'll take your blood pressure and temperature and make sure the doctor comes in right away." Faith did the routine tasks while trying to remember when she noticed the flag had been flipped. She made it a habit to look down the hallway every time she went in or out of an exam room, or updated files from her computer, set in the alcove of the hallway. It had not been extended when she had helped with the last patient in exam room four. How could she have missed it?

The woman was just as scathing with the doctor when he arrived. He soothed her and told her how things could get backed up with no warning and he also apologized. Once she left, however, he questioned Faith.

"I don't know how I missed it. I'm sorry. It won't happen again," she said, trying to remember if she'd somehow overlooked the fact that the flag had been out.

"Daydreaming about the sheriff, I expect," Marjorie murmured as she passed them in the hallway.

"What's that?" the doctor asked.

Marjorie shrugged. "Our Faith has her eye set on Tate Johnson and spends more time mooning about that than work," she said.

"That's not true on any level," Faith protested. She looked at the doctor. "I do not shirk my responsibilities, nor forget what's going on by daydreaming. And I'm not after Tate."

"Then how do you explain forgetting about Mrs. Foster?" she asked.

She looked at Marjorie, suspecting what had happened. "I can't. I'll make sure it doesn't happen again," she said.

"No harm done," the doctor said. "Muriel Foster does like to have her way. Are the McCrackin twins in?"

"In the waiting room," Marjorie said. "Is an exam room ready for them?"

"Exam room three is ready," Faith said. She tried to keep her composure, sure the older woman had deliberately postponed extending the flag until the patient had waited long enough to become angry. But there was no way to prove it and in a case of a newcomer's word against a longtime employee's, she knew she'd look like she was trying to dodge the blame.

The rest of the day Faith checked each exam room when she walked by, to make sure it was empty if it was flagged as empty. But the stress of Marjorie's actions was getting to her.

How long would it take the receptionist to get over the fact that Faith had the job her niece had vied for?

By afternoon, Faith couldn't wait to leave work. Two more patients had commented on her dating the sheriff. She'd overheard Marjorie making one of her snide comments and now knew where the rumors had started. Beyond refuting that they were dating, she could do nothing to stop the gossip. Only time would let the topic die out as a new one caught the interest of the town's residents.

Doubly conscious of the rumors Marjorie was spreading, Faith didn't want to feed them by being seen around town with Tate. She left a message for him at the sheriff's office, saying she'd meet him at the singles meeting. When she arrived, he was not there. She gravitated toward Janette and Peter, and they discussed the items that had been donated and made a preliminary plan to pick up what they could for the sale.

Tate still had not arrived when the pastor joined them for the Bible study. Faith wondered where he was and gave a quick prayer that he was all right. Something had probably come up. When her phone vibrated a few minutes into the study, she noted that the number was the clinic. Excusing herself, she hurried outside the fellowship hall to answer.

"Bad accident on one of the rural roads. The sheriff's department is bringing in two injured. I'll need your help here," Dr. Mallory said.

"I'm at the church—I'll be there in less than five minutes," she responded. She went back inside to get her purse and explain briefly that she was needed and left. Walking rapidly, she reached the clinic in minutes. The lights were on and the door unlocked.

"Dr. Mallory?" she called.

"Back here, getting things ready."

She went back and saw exam room one's door open, the doctor inside laying out a tray of bandages and instruments.

Quickly, she put away her purse and slipped on a

tunic she kept in her drawer. It would have to do—she didn't have time to get home and into a uniform.

"Do you know what happened?" she asked.

"Some fool was driving his truck too fast," he said. "Lost control around the curve near the Hendricks' farm and smashed into a tree. Two injured, both teenagers. Sheriff's Department's notifying the parents, and they'll meet us here. We're doing triage. If they need more care, we'll transport to the hospital in Monkesville."

In no time, the fire department's ambulance pulled up by the front door. The EMTs jumped to the ground and pulled out one gurney with a young woman strapped on for safety. A moment later, they helped a teenage boy out of the back and walked with him into the clinic.

The next half hour was busy with X-rays and sutures, pain meds doled out, and dealing with parents frantic with worry about their children. Faith was conscious of Tate's presence, the bloody smears on his uniform attesting to his help at the scene. His demeanor calmed the parents. His steady assurances had them feeling better about the situation. And when both teens were given the okay to return home, they thanked the sheriff, the doctor and Faith. And the young man's parents began telling the boy what the consequences were going to be, now that they knew he was safe.

Tate came to the exam room when everyone had left. "Sorry about missing tonight's meeting. We got the call just as I was starting out."

"I wondered where you were," she said as she began cleaning the exam room. Tate leaned against the doorjamb.

"It could've been worse. At least they were both wearing seat belts," he said, idly watching her work.

"Thank the Lord for that."

"I did. And that we got notified right away. I doubt either would have bled out, but we strive for speedy responses to accidents." He glanced at her. "The Hendricks' dog was barking and wouldn't stop, so he went out to see why. Spotted the truck and called it in."

"I'm glad neither of them was seriously injured. And it might be a good thing in the long run—they'll both think twice about driving too fast in the future," Faith said.

She turned and stopped, since Tate blocked the door. "I need to clean up the other room before I go," she said.

He nodded and stepped back into the hall, glancing at his clothes. "Pretty gross," he said.

"I've seen worse," she said, passing him to get to the next room.

Tate followed and again stood in the doorway.

"I need to get home and shower and change," he said.

He met her eyes.

"I'm fine here, if you're just waiting until I leave."

"I'll wait until you lock up. Then drive you home."

"Not necessary. No need to give rise to gossip." She tried to maintain her resolve to keep a distance between them until the rumors died down.

"We can turn out all the lights, sneak to the patrol car. It has tinted windows—no one will see," he teased, watching her closely.

Faith laughed. "Okay, maybe I'm overreacting, but every third person who came to the clinic today had a comment about you and me. I think Marjorie is fueling the gossip, and I wish she'd stop."

"Again…why do we care? We know the truth."

"Which is?"

"I like being with you, you like being with me. We have a good friendship," he responded.

"Umm." Hard to refute, except, in all honesty, there was an awareness that could definitely spill over to stronger feelings, if she let it. Which she wouldn't do.

"Okay, let's sneak out," she said, still smiling at the thought.

Tate enjoyed that she was amused by his comment. He liked seeing her happy and laughing. Especially after the gruesome cleanup she'd had to do tonight. Those kids were lucky they hadn't been injured more seriously.

The drive home was short. Faith insisted she'd be fine getting up the steps to her apartment. Tate stood by the patrol car until she was inside, then headed for the station. He wanted to write up the report and double-check that the truck had been towed. He had a change of clothes at the station and could shower there.

He hoped the gossips would find something else to chew on and leave Faith alone. Until then, he'd do his bit by staying away.

Until Saturday's barbecue.

Faith drove to the Johnsons' home Saturday afternoon. She had butterflies as she parked on the street, already crowded with cars, and walked to the house. The day was perfect. The sun shone from a cloudless sky, and there was enough air stirring to keep the temperature comfortable. Hearing the laughter and murmur of conversations from the rear, she walked around the side and stopped. It seemed as if half of Rocky Point was present in the large yard. There was a huge brick barbecue near the back of the house, already smoking. A cement patio about the size of a football field was full of picnic tables, folding chairs, huge umbrellas and people. Large covered bowls and trays of goodies filled two tables sitting in the shade of the house.

She was questioning whether this had been such a good idea when Cecile Johnson spotted her.

"Faith, welcome. Come on over. So glad you could come." Cecile's warm welcome chased away the trace of shyness.

Faith greeted her hostess with a smile. "Is half the town here?" she asked, glancing around. Where was Tate?

"Only seems like it sometimes," Cecile said with a laugh. "Come on, I'll introduce you around."

Within minutes, Faith felt even more connected. Turned out, she knew more people than not. Some were patients, others she had met through Trinity Church, a few she'd chatted with at the ice-cream parlor.

"You know Marcie," Cecile said as they approached the café owner.

"Of course. I enjoy her restaurant probably more than I should."

"Hey, always glad to welcome customers," Marcie replied, giving Faith a quick hug. "Anyway, today's a treat, I don't have to worry about a thing."

"Oh, excuse me, I see the Overtons," Cecile said, giving Faith a little pat on her shoulder.

"Drinks are in the coolers near the barbecue. I think Todd puts them there so he gets to see everyone. Otherwise, he'd miss people, chained to the barbecue as he is."

"Can't someone else help?" Faith asked Marcie as they walked his way.

"No way. Todd would never let anyone else approach his barbecue. We were so worried the year he had his stroke that this event would be canceled." She grinned. "He did allow Tate to help that year. A one-time-only deal, though. Hey, Todd, Faith just got here."

"Hi, Faith. Help yourself to a drink. We'll start serving the ribs in about an hour."

Marcie and Faith wandered from group to group, chatting with neighbors, laughing with friends. Faith loved that fact everyone seemed to know each other and mingled so well.

She still hadn't seen Tate. Had he been unable to attend?

"There's Zack. He and his car club. Honestly, you'd think a retired race-car driver could stay away from the track," Marcie said in fond exasperation.

Faith nodded and looked over toward the spot in the yard Marcie indicated. Zack Kincaid was surrounded by excited, chattering teenagers, and Tate stood beside him with an indulgent expression on his face. When Zack spotted Marcie, he said something and then walked directly toward her. Everyone laughed. Tate stayed where he was, but looked over and gave a wave to Faith. She waved back.

"Tell me more about the car club," she said when Zack joined them. He put his arm around Marcie's shoulders.

"Zack started it to help out Sean, a local teenager. Tate was instrumental in getting him connected with a place large enough to have a track," Marcie explained.

"At first they wanted to race. But the parking lot we took over isn't conducive to that. So now we have an obstacle course, and parking spots and contests to see who can drive the best—or park the quickest—things like that. Each kid has to have a note from his or her parents to participate," Zack added.

"And when school starts, they have to keep up their grades," Marcie chimed in. "That was Tate's idea."

"Yeah, I just wanted them to learn driving safety," Zack said, smiling down at Marcie.

Faith was taken aback by the pure love shining in his eyes. Glancing at Marcie, she saw it reflected in hers. She had once thought she and Allen had shared such a connection.

"Glad you came," Tate said, drawing her attention away from the other two a second later. "Meet Sean O'Connell. Sean, this is Faith Stewart. She's the new nurse at the clinic."

"Nice to meet you," Sean said, holding out his hand.

"I hear you are the one who got the car club started," she said to the teenager as she shook his hand.

"Naw, Zack did. It's great."

"Go get your drink and take some back to the rest of the kids," Tate suggested. Sean nodded and took off.

"Sorry I wasn't here when you arrived. Mom introduce you around?"

"Yes. Then Marcie took over. So, were you at the car club this morning?"

"Yeah, I go as often as I can. Keeps the kids on their toes. Come with me—I need a drink. It's hotter today than I expected." They walked to the coolers. Tate greeted his dad, offered to help and was firmly refused. The sheriff smiled and shrugged.

"The car club sounds awesome," she said as they

drifted toward the edge of the patio to stand beneath one of the large umbrellas.

"It's definitely gone a long way in teaching kids about responsible driving," Tate said. "And it helps that everyone thinks Zack is some kind of hero."

"Hero?"

"He's a grand prix racer—won a lot of races. Well known for that."

"Umm." She turned to look for him in the crowd. He was still with Marcie, and a couple of others. He looked right at home.

Jenny came running over. "Hi, Faith. How's my puppy?"

"Doing great. Are you coming tomorrow after church to see her?"

"Yes. And Melissa and Sally Anne, too. If that's okay."

Faith smiled. "It sure is. I'll have snacks."

"You're the greatest! Hi, Sheriff Tate. Are you getting a puppy, too?" Jenny asked.

"I'm afraid I'm away from home too much," he said.

"You can come visit mine when I get her," Jenny offered.

"Thanks. I'd like that."

She grinned, then dashed away to rejoin the kids playing on the grass some distance away. Faith counted ten boys and girls around Jenny's age, but wasn't sure she included everyone since they were playing tag and running back and forth, laughing and shouting.

The girls must have said something, because a minute later two young boys came running straight toward them.

"Sheriff, my mom said I can go on the tour," said one of the boys, out of breath when he stopped in front of Tate. He breathed hard for a minute. "But it has to be on a Saturday—I can't miss school. That starts in two weeks. Can we do it on a Saturday?"

"Sure thing, Jimbo. Want to firm up a date now? I can't make it for the next few Saturdays. How about the Saturday after the Kincaid wedding, at ten?"

"Okay, I'll tell my mom."

"And me, too, Sheriff?" the other boy asked, his eyes shining with hope.

"Of course, Will." Tate said. The boys high-fived each other and the sheriff. Then they plunged into the group on the patio, searching for their mothers.

"What was that about?" Faith asked, once again seeing how well he interacted with children. How sad that he and his wife had not had a child before her illness.

"Periodically, we give tours of the station. Nothing impressive, like in Boston, but it's part of a program set up with the school. We hope to give the kids a good understanding of the department, and slip in a few cautionary reminders, as well."

"I'm sure they're thrilled."

"I don't know…I think they like the fire-department tour more. Even I liked that one better."

Faith nodded with a grin. "I would, too. Especially if I could make the siren sound."

"Hey, police cars have sirens, too, you know."

She quirked a brow. "Oh, so can I sound the siren if I sign up for a tour?"

"You could go on a ride-along and, maybe on some quiet road with no one around to get spooked, you can sound the siren as much as you like. I'll take you tonight," he said, his eyes staring into hers.

Faith's heart skipped a beat. "Sounds like a plan, Sheriff."

She wasn't going to call it a date. But she looked forward to their time alone as much as she enjoyed his company now.

Tate and Faith walked around, talking with other guests, enjoying the food when it was served.

Faith wished she'd had today's barbecue before her dinner with her friend, Helen. She'd seen her oncologist for her semiannual checkup Wednesday and then met Helen for dinner at a restaurant in Portland they both liked. It had been a fun meal of catching up. Helen was fascinated by Faith's description of the small town. She'd have to remember the details of the summer barbecue to regale her friend the next time they met.

"Don't you ever miss Portland?" Helen had asked at one point.

Faith had considered the question a long moment before responding. "Not at all. Maybe my friends like you, but everything is new and different and I'm finding a spot for myself unlike anything here."

At one point in the evening Helen had casually mentioned seeing Allen. Faith had been surprised to realize she didn't care at all. The ache and hurt from his betrayal had faded.

Or was it because of the man standing next to her today?

She was afraid she was becoming too attached to Tate Johnson. That would never do. She could be in for a major heartbreak if she fell in love with the sheriff. A man couldn't make it much clearer that he was not in the market for a relationship.

Which still struck her as too bad, given how well

he did with children. He'd make a great father. Children would be blessed to have him as their dad. She wished her own parents had lived long enough for her to remember them. She told herself they loved her, but she had nothing to base that on. Tate was easygoing with friends and family. Still, when the job demanded it, he could be hard as nails. A good combination for law enforcement.

The barbecue didn't end until after dark. Faith was amazed at the amount of food the guests consumed and that more kept appearing. She wondered how that worked.

As families began to gather their kids and head out, Tate nudged Faith. "Want to sound that siren?"

"I need to check on Maggie first. I didn't know I'd be gone this long. Poor dog—she's probably crossing her legs by now."

"I'll follow you home. You can take her for a walk and feed her and then we'll find a quiet street off in the boonies where you can turn on the siren."

She smiled as she looked at him. "Is this really silly?"

"Hey, as a kid I always wanted to drive fast and have the siren going. Why do you think I became a cop?"

She laughed at that. She was laughing a lot around Tate. She liked it. "I think for one or two other reasons, but if that's what floats your boat, it's as good a reason as any."

Tate had not driven a police car to the picnic, so while Faith was taking care of her dog, he went to the station. Checking that things were quiet, he told the dispatcher he'd take a quick patrol out to Carlisle Beach and back. Since he did this throughout the summer, she didn't think anything of it. Tate knew it was more to give Faith the chance to ride in the police car than to check that anything was going on at Carlisle Beach. On Labor Day, the church end-of-summer picnic would be held there. Until then, lots of tourists enjoyed the wide sandy beach.

Faith was waiting on the steps when he drove up. She came to the driver's side and leaned against the window, bending over to see him. "Is this legal?"

"We give ride-alongs all the time. All the rage."

"Can I get a tour of the station when Jimbo and the other boy go?" she asked.

He grinned. "You can have a tour any time you want."

"Deal." She ran around the car and slipped into the passenger side. "When can I push the button on the siren?" she asked.

"I'll let you know."

Tate headed for the beach, driving along the back roads. Once far enough from houses to not bother anyone, he gave her the go-ahead. Faith flipped the switch and the siren sounded loud and long.

"Oh, wow, it's so loud!' she exclaimed. "I thought it wouldn't blare so much in the car." Fumbling, she switched it off. "Thanks. I'll probably be half-deaf for the next week. But that was fun. I'd run it all the time if I were a cop."

"No, you wouldn't. It's not as loud if the windows are closed. But we want people to hear it, you know."

There were two groups at the beach, two fires going for warmth and illumination. Everyone was having a good time and there was no need for Tate to do more than drive by. Then he had an idea. Driving farther along the shore, he came to the lookout point for the town. Carlisle Beach was at the center of a large cove, horseshoe shaped, with Rocky Point at one end and the lookout at another.

He pulled to a stop. "Come on, this'll be pretty," he said, getting out of the car. They walked to the rail. Before them lay the dark sea, shimmering here and there as it reflected the moon. The bonfires looked like small dots of light. In the distance the lights of the town flickered.

They went to stand near the guardrail, looking at the glittering lights in the distance.

"It's beautiful," Faith said.

The moon was rising in the dark sky, so bright it outshone the nearby stars. The light glimmered on the ocean where the small waves skimmed across. The lights from Rocky Point sparkled in the distance.

Tate put his foot on the rail, leaning on his upraised knee. "I like this view. It's really something in winter, when the town decorates for Christmas. Then you can see all the colors."

Faith stood quietly by his side, staring at the view. For a moment, Tate felt a sense of contentment seep in. He looked to the sky and gave a quick thanks for the day, for a gathering of friends both old and new.

"I had fun at the picnic. I knew more people than I expected," she said.

"Sooner or later, you'll get to know everyone when they come through the clinic."

"Umm. Are you going to the church picnic at the beach?" she asked. The singles had other plans. She was torn about which event to attend.

"No, I'm on duty, and took enough time today for my folks's event. I'll be on patrol. Might drive that way for a quick check."

"I'm not sure I'm going. I feel bad being gone all day and leaving Maggie at home alone. And she can't go and leave those puppies so long. Do people take dogs on picnics?"

"A bunch do." He put his foot back on the ground and turned to her. "Are you getting tired?"

"A little. I'm still not up to full strength yet."

"I'll take you home."

She reached out her hand to touch his arm. "I've had a wonderful day. Thank you."

"It was fun, wasn't it?" Then he leaned over and kissed her gently on the lips. A brief kiss, over almost before it began. He pulled back, not knowing whether to apologize or go for a second one.

She stepped back and turned toward the car.

"I was out of line," he said, following her quickly. What had he done? He didn't want to give anyone false expectations. He was not looking for any long-term relationship, not looking to fall in love. And kissing nice girls like Faith would definitely raise expectations. Plus, they'd discussed the no-romance aspect. He felt like an idiot.

"I'm sorry," he said as he opened the car door for her.

"It's okay. Just a kiss between friends." The words sounded right, but she didn't look at him. Even once they were both in the car, she kept her face slightly averted.

"It won't happen again," he said. Had he blown everything?

The smile looked forced, even to him. "It's fine, Tate."

The silence in the car on the ride back to town was deafening. He couldn't think of anything else to say, nothing to excuse his blunder. He'd wanted to kiss her and had, and it now looked like he'd damaged their budding friendship.

"Want me to walk with you and Maggie?" he asked when they reached her apartment.

"No, we'll be fine. I keep the walks short this late. Thanks again."

He walked her up to the door. She unlocked it to the welcoming bark. Maggie had mastered the art of jumping the barrier and came rushing to the door, dancing around in her delight to see them.

"Hey, girl, how're you doing?" Tate asked, kneeling down to pet her, holding her away as she tried to lick his face.

Faith stood watching them. Tate wished he knew what she was thinking.

He rose to his feet. "Well, then, good night."

She nodded and then surprised him by reaching out to touch his cheek. "I really did have a great day," she said softly. "Kiss and all."

With that she went quickly inside and called Maggie.

Tate watched the door close, trying to figure out where he stood. *Kiss and all.* Maybe she wasn't upset about the kiss. Maybe she didn't expect wedding bells because of one kiss.

He drove home and went inside, feeling oddly defensive. Glancing at Mandy's picture, guilt struck. He walked over. How could he kiss someone else when his wife had meant so much to him?

"Hey," he said to the photograph. He stared at her for a long time. He'd loved her. She had loved him. And had told him more than once that he was not to mourn forever, but go on with life. God was taking her, but sparing him. So that meant He had great plans for Tate. She wanted him to be happy.

"I was so happy with you," he said sadly. Then a comment Faith had made earlier caused him to smile. "I think I'm getting happy with Faith. I think you would like her. She's got the most infectious laugh. Her whole face seems to light up and her eyes sparkle."

He knew Mandy couldn't speak to him, but he knew what she'd say.

"I'm afraid to reach out for that life you told me to. What if I fall for another woman and she gets sick and dies? I don't think I could bear that again."

Unceasing faith. The message from Pastor John echoed. What Tate needed to do was step out in unceasing faith and discover what the Lord had planned for him. If only he was brave enough.

Chapter Seven

Faith enjoyed church the next morning. She was getting better at finding passages in the Bible when the pastor referred to them. The hymns were her delight. As was the warmth she felt being greeted by more and more people each Sunday. She didn't see Tate, for which she had mixed emotions. She'd thought about that kiss all night. It had been spur of the moment. She knew it had been a whim. He had been clear from their first interaction that he loved his dead wife. He was not going to rush into another relationship. Especially with someone like her.

Not that he'd said that in so many words, but she knew. No family to speak of. Being unable to bear children. And she knew she was still at risk for a recurrence. She was two years cancer-free, but that didn't mean cured.

Help me face reality, Father, she prayed silently as the organ music welcomed those to the service. *I need to know where You want me. I think it's here. Can I be a help to this community? Find lasting friends who will accept me as I am? Not yearn for the closeness of a mate, a family. There is so much I can do. Help me see that, and not my own wishes.*

Not wish a certain handsome sheriff would throw caution to the wind and court her. Not wish she could have a baby to hold, to love. Not wish for a future secure in love.

She had the Father's love. As peace descended, she knew it was more than enough.

When the service ended, Faith was soon surrounded by singles group members. Once again, they met for lunch on Marcie's restaurant's patio. Faith wondered what they did in the winter. She planned to find out.

The talk centered around their own picnic on Labor Day.

"So you don't go with the rest of the church?" Faith asked.

"We have in the past, and it's fun. But last year we held our own gathering at the marina park. No kids running around, no sand in the shoes," Stan explained.

Faith grinned. "Are you getting old, Stan? That's part of the fun of going to the beach."

"Yeah, well, we all had fun and got home at a reasonable hour. We all had work the next day, you know."

"I think the beach's more fun if you're going swimming, and I'm not going in that cold water," Dana said.

"The kids do," Janette remarked.

"I did, too, when I was that young. I think kids don't have an internal thermostat. They're fine in freezing water."

"Count me in. I was hesitant about going to the beach because of being away from my dog for so long," Faith said.

"But you can bring her to the marina park—that's close enough. We'd love to see her," Janette said.

"Wish you could bring the puppies," Stan added.

"That would be a disaster. When I first found them, I could pick them up and they just sort of snuggled closer. Now they are bundles of energy, not wanting to be held, wanting to explore, chase each other, pounce." She smiled ruefully. "They're so funny, but the bigger they get, the more I look forward to weaning them and placing them in their new homes."

"So let's plan on what we're each bringing," Dana said, steering the conversation back to the picnic.

"What should I bring?" Faith asked. It would be a smaller gathering than the church picnic, and easier to get to and leave if she became tired.

"Potato salad. Stan's bringing hot dogs and hamburgers, Pete's bringing his famous coleslaw, I'm bringing dessert and a couple of the others are bringing fruit, chips and sodas." She paused. "How about noon? We'll stake the place out earlier to make sure we have a couple of picnic tables and celebrate together when we all show up."

"Shall I bring horseshoes?" Stan asked.

"Of course," Janette said, grinning. "I want a rematch." She looked at Faith. "Stan beat the socks off all of us last year. I think he practices all year long to be reigning champion."

"I've never played," Faith said.

"Oh, be prepared to be beaten," Stan teased.

Faith began to look forward to the event. This group of singles were longtime friends. They did fun things together. She'd never heard any of them bemoaning that they weren't married. Except for Dorothy, who was widowed and still missed her husband. Faith planned to spend more time with them, to see how they accepted life as the Lord had laid out.

That afternoon Gillian brought Jenny and her two friends to see the puppies.

"Come in and visit while they play," Faith said.

"I'd love to just sit and veg out," Gillian said fervently. "Honestly, getting ready for a wedding is lots more work than I thought it would be. What happened to two people standing in front of the pastor and exchanging vows?"

"Isn't that what you're doing?" Faith asked as she went to get them iced tea. The girls were rolling around on the kitchen floor, giggling in delight, puppies everywhere.

Sitting beside Gillian on the sofa a moment later, Faith tilted her head slightly and looked at her new friend. "So what's going on that has you so stressed?"

"Everything. Will the flowers arrive on time? Will there be enough food for the reception? What if it rains?"

"But no second thoughts?" Faith asked.

Gillian looked at her and shook her head slowly. "No second thoughts at all. I love Joe to pieces. I can't wait until we're married and living together and sharing every aspect of our lives. It's just that the wedding's like this big hurdle to overcome. If I can just last until next Sunday, I'll be okay." She took a long drink of the iced tea. "You never responded to the invitation. Are you coming?"

Faith blinked. "I didn't get an invitation."

"Of course you did. I wouldn't leave you out. Especially with what's going on between you and Tate. I gave it to Marjorie a week or so ago, when I brought

Jenny in for her school checkup. I didn't see you in that madhouse, so asked her to give it to you."

"Oh. I guess she forgot." Faith knew that was not the case, but expected Marjorie would come up with some excuse if challenged about it.

"I can't believe it! I thought you got it that day. Anyway, you're coming, right?"

"I'd like that," Faith said. And realized it was true. The pain of her own aborted plans had diminished. She could rejoice with her new friend and find pleasure in her wedding to the man she loved. No reason for her to neglect a friend's happiness just because Allen had turned out to be a poor choice.

"Good. It turns out I'm going to have plenty of people sitting on my side. I thought at first that everyone in town would come because of Joe." She glanced at Faith. "His family's been here forever. But several of my clients said they're coming because of me."

"Joe's family's been here that long?" Faith asked.

"Mine, too, though I didn't know that until after I moved here last April. Several of the families around here were settlers in the wild country. This was all Massachusetts back before the Revolution. They fought side by side against the British." A reflective light filled her eyes. "I wonder what would have happened if I'd been raised here instead of Nevada? Maybe Joe and I would have met years ago and have a houseful of kids by now. But I don't think that was the Lord's plan. This is."

"You speak with such assurance."

"You should have seen me a few months ago. Uncertain about everything. But now I have a feeling of rightness about everything. We've prayed about it and we both believe this is the way the Lord wants us to go."

"I'm still searching," Faith said slowly.

A burst of laughter from the kitchen had her involuntarily smiling as she turned to see what the girls were doing. Obviously, the puppies were still a big hit.

"Seek ye first the kingdom of God," Gillian quoted softly.

"I am. It's still new to me, but I find more and more confidence in the direction I think the Lord is leading me as I settle in here."

"You have many friends who like you a lot. Just think, in the years ahead, my kids can play with yours, we'll grow old together and remember back when I was a nervous wreck about my wedding and you were the newcomer to town."

Faith didn't say anything. She wasn't going to explode Gillian's wishful thinking today. She hoped Gillian and new husband had a house full of kids. Maybe she could go over to see them, just as Jenny came to visit with the puppies.

Labor Day dawned to a clear sky and warm temperatures. Faith prepared potato salad—enough for everyone she expected at the picnic. She gathered her things and brought Maggie with her to the park. The puppies were contained, and were getting used to their mama being gone for short periods. She was close enough to take Maggie home when she'd had enough, but Faith wanted to show off her dog to her friends.

Stan arrived first and laid claim to two of the picnic tables that were close together. Faith joined him, placing her bowl on one table.

"You picked the best ones. They'll be shady all day."

"I hope so. I've been here two hours already."

She laughed, glancing around. Other groups were arriving, staking claims to tables. Soon the park would be full. Then picnickers would have to set up on the grass. "Good move. Here come Peter and Dana."

Soon most of the members of the singles group had arrived. Faith didn't expect Tate to join them—she knew he had to work today. But she wouldn't let that interfere with her enjoying her new friends. Lively discussions ensued. There was a lot of laughter, and everyone made a big to-do over Maggie. She wagged her tail nonstop.

"What a love. Is this the one who had puppies?" Rachel asked. "I might like one as a guard dog for the antiques shop."

Faith shook her head. "Unless you want burglars licked to death, I'm not sure that would be a wise move. These are the sweetest dogs you'll ever meet."

"Oh, well, then just for companionship. You're a lot of fun, aren't you, Maggie?" she crooned to the dog, scratching behind her ears.

Maggie almost purred she was so delighted.

"I'm sold. Keep one of the puppies for me," Rachel said.

"That's the lot, then. She only had four puppies and three are already spoken for, so you'll get the last one."

"Oh, good! Who else is getting them?"

"Jenny Kincaid was the first. Then a couple of her friends. We've talked about going to obedience-training classes together. In Monkesville. Though Tate suggested we see about having the trainer come here once a week if we got enough people interested."

"Oh, if it works with my schedule, count me in. If the dog's so sweet, he can stay at the shop with me. I love places that have pets there to greet customers," Rachel said.

"I'll let you know," Faith promised.

Stan put the charcoal in the barbecue grill between the tables and soon had the coals glowing. "Bring on the meat," he called. Two of the other men joined him while the rest of the group congregated around one of the tables.

"Grilling outdoors is not only a man's chore," one of the women called over.

The men around the grill waved the comment away to the merriment of everyone.

Faith was enjoying herself, though she couldn't help looking at the road when a car drove by, hoping Tate would find a couple of minutes to stop by.

Janette noticed and grinned. "He'll come if he can," she said, leaning closer so only Faith could hear.

"Who?" she asked, which made Janette giggle.

"As if you don't know."

Myra Simpson arrived then. She was one of the older members of the group. "I need help," she called. Immediately everyone scrambled off the benches and hurried to her car.

"I brought an old-fashioned ice-cream maker, rock salt, ingredients and ice. The ice is in the cooler."

"Fabulous idea," someone said, reaching out to take one handle of the cooler. Someone else took the other and they lifted it from the trunk, carrying it over to the tables. The rest of the items were gathered up to bring to their picnic area.

Faith was excited at the thought of homemade ice cream. She didn't think she'd ever had it before. There were so many new things for her to experience in her adopted hometown. She was delighted she'd made the move.

"I'm going to take Maggie home. I'll be right back," she said, still by Myra's car. There were more and more people in the park now. Plus, the puppies would be wondering where their mama was.

When she returned to the park, the first of the grilled hot dogs and hamburgers were being served. After the blessing was said, the entire group began eating.

Faith offered to crank the ice-cream maker a half hour later. It got harder and harder with each turn of the crank. Others urged her on, but she was glad when Janette said it was her turn. They all wanted to help make the treat. Her arm was aching, but she was glad to have the experience.

Just then, Tate walked across the grass toward them. Her heart raced and she felt as if the day gained brighter color than before. She couldn't help the smile of welcome on her face.

"Hi, Tate," one of the others called. "You're right on time."

He nodded, his gaze sweeping the group, settling on Faith. He smiled. "Making ice cream?"

"Yes, and it's not as easy as it looks."

"Harder to crank the more the cream becomes solid," he said.

"You've done this before," she said, stepping closer, happy he'd been able to stop by.

"Every summer as a kid. My dad always had to finish it. Once we were grown, I think he was glad to give it up."

"Let the sheriff have a turn," Stan said. "I have a couple of burgers left. Want something to eat?"

"Sure. I'll get it."

Faith went with him as he dished up a plate and sat at one of the tables. "So is everything peaceful today?" she asked.

"So far. Parties everywhere, though. Which could lead to drinking and an altercation or two tonight. But I always hope for the best. Having fun?"

"Oh, yes." Faith looked around. No one else had come to the table. Everyone was still by the ice-cream maker, laughing as each new person had more and more trouble cranking the handle.

"I found it hard going when I was doing it," she said, laughing at Janette's grimace as she tried to turn the handle. "I can't wait to taste it. Peach ice cream, with cut-up chunks of peaches," she explained.

"Myra's favorite," he said, then took another bite of his hamburger.

"Guess what? Rachel's taking the last puppy. Once they're weaned, they'll all have good homes. Then I'm having Maggie spayed."

"Good idea. One of my deputies talked to a woman who does obedience training. He asked her if she'd give a couple of classes in Rocky Point. There could be a lot of folks who would participate. She said if there were fifteen or more, she'd do it."

"Rachel's interested, and the girls and me. With other dog owners, we could end up with that many. I'll ask around. Maybe Dr. Mallory would let me post a sign at the clinic."

"We'll post one at the station, and try the ice-cream shop. They're good about supporting local events."

Tate finished eating just as Myra declared the ice cream ready. Everyone had a small serving and pronounced it the best ice cream ever. He liked watching Faith as she discovered the joy of homemade ice cream. She seemed to blossom in this group. Her laughter was infectious. Her eyes were a bright blue, shining with happiness. He could watch her all day.

Which wasn't possible. Checking his watch, he noted that he'd spent almost an hour at the picnic. Time to get back on rounds.

"I've got to go," he said, rising and putting the paper bowl in the trash. Did he imagine it, or did Faith look disappointed?

"Glad you could join us, if only for a little while," she said.

"Me, too." He wished he could reach out and touch her. Spend more of the day with her. Enjoy her company as the rest of the group would be able to all afternoon. Duty called, however.

As he drove through town, he questioned his own feelings. Before meeting Faith, he had been certain he would never fall in love again. That he couldn't risk his heart on losing someone he loved. But now, she brought sunlight and happiness into his life. Just being with her gave him a feeling of joy. Maybe the Lord was telling him it was not set in stone that he not remarry.

Whoa, *remarry?* He didn't want to think that far ahead. Right now he just wanted to spend time with her. Get to know her better. See what developed between them. He knew enough of her history to recognize that he had better be one hundred percent certain of what he wanted before speaking to her. He would never want to be a man who would let her down, as her former fiancé had.

So maybe he'd better take things slower. Be sure. Give her time to know what she wanted. Give himself time to know what he wanted. She had fought cancer and won. What if it came back? Could he deal with that a second time?

Tate didn't like himself much when he considered that he might wish to run from such a situation. But how could he stay around and watch her waste away as Mandy had? His gut twisted at the thought.

Lord, Your will be done. If Faith's the one for me, give me the strength to claim her, love her and build a future for us together, whatever comes.

The next morning Faith walked to work. Already she could see the change in Rocky Point. There was hardly a soul out and about. Unlike every other day she'd been there, when families and groups of kids had been all over. School started today. Visitors had returned home. Now she'd get to experience the Rocky Point of residents only.

She was the first to reach the clinic and walked through, turning on lights, opening the doors to the exam rooms. They had been prepared Saturday before she left, but she wanted to make sure everything was ready for the day.

Exam room two had no paper supplies. Faith frowned. Everything had been set on Saturday. She checked in the cupboard beneath the sink. None there, either. She sighed. Going to the supply closet in the back, she gathered paper towels, a roll of paper that went on the exam table, wipes and a box of tissue. Once the room had been taken care of, she checked the others to make sure nothing was missing. All seemed in order.

She walked to the front. Enough was enough. When Marjorie arrived this morning, Faith was going to have it out with her.

Please, Lord, give me the right words. I want to work harmoniously with everyone. Please let me get through to her. Even if I leave, it doesn't mean the doctor will hire her niece, does it? But this has to stop.

She raised the blinds in the reception area. In no time patients would arrive and the day would begin. She hoped Marjorie would arrive early. She was not going to put up with her recalcitrant attitude any longer.

Idly, she straightened the reception desk. There was a pink message slip partially beneath the blotter. She pulled it out, seeing her name. Her oncologist had called last week. A feeling of dread engulfed her when she saw the note—*anomalies.*

She swallowed hard, the words blurring. Anomalies in her test results. Her heart pounded. Did that mean the cancer had returned? She swallowed hard. Oh, please, not that.

She sank down in the chair, staring at the pink slip. She was a nurse. She knew the terminology used to soften diagnoses. *Anomalies* sounded better than a *problem.* But it was the same thing.

Marjorie would be here any moment. Suddenly her petty harassments faded in importance. Faith jumped up and went to the back. There was a phone at the small area by her computer. She quickly called the doctor's office. Why hadn't Marjorie made sure she got this last week? How cruel to sit on it for days on end.

"Dr. Stephens's exchange," said the voice answering the call.

"I need to speak to Dr. Stephens," Faith said, trying to keep the panic from her voice.

"I'm sorry, the doctor's on vacation. Dr. Hutchins is handling his calls. He'll be in the office at nine."

"What about Dr. Stephens's nurse?" she asked. She could give Faith the information.

"The medical office is closed for two weeks. Dr. Hutchins is handling all calls."

"Okay, give me his number and I'll call at nine." That was only a half hour away. An endless half hour waiting to hear the results of her tests. Her heart sank. Tears blurred her eyes. She thought she was cured.

Help me, please, Father God. I'm so scared. I thought I was healed. Your power can heal everything. If it's Your will, please make me better. For a long moment she stared off to nothing. *But if not, then maybe my time here is over. Thank You for the blessings I've had so far.*

She felt numb. Vaguely she heard Marjorie come in. A few minutes later Dr. Mallory arrived.

"Good morning, Faith. I expect our days will be a little quieter now that the kids are in school and the tourists are gone," he said in passing.

"Good morning," she responded. She wanted to blurt out the situation. But held back. She didn't know the prognosis. *Anomalies.* It couldn't be good, however.

It was well after nine before Faith had a chance to call Dr. Hutchins's office.

"Sorry, the doctor is with a patient, can I help?" his receptionist said.

Faith explained things to her, but was told she'd have to speak to the doctor. The woman took Faith's phone number and promised to give it to the doctor as soon as he was free.

The morning dragged by. At her lunch break, Faith

dashed home. She walked Maggie, watching the dog with a heavy heart. She loved this dog. But if the cancer had returned, and she needed to go through chemotherapy again, she wouldn't have the energy to keep up with a young, healthy dog. Maggie loved walks, runs. How could she deal with that? She had been so enervated the last time she'd had chemo treatment.

Standing at the park she looked around, memories flooding in. The picnic had been so much fun. Meeting Tate here a couple of times gave her good memories. The contentment she felt sitting on the bench and gazing at the sea seemed far-off today.

Tate.

Her heart dropped. She couldn't let him know. He'd been so devastated by his wife's illness and death. She couldn't let him know. He thought he'd run if he were ever faced with such a situation again. But she didn't think so. How could she expect him—even as a friend—to stand by and watch her fight the cancer again. Every setback would remind him of Mandy's losing battle.

She sat on a bench. "I'm not sure I'm up to that," she said softly, gazing at the sea. "Maybe this is just the way things are supposed to be."

She'd have to return to Portland. There were no facilities here to deal with the treatment that would be required. She'd see if she could find a small place near the hospital. She knew all too well how hard it was to do things when she had no energy. Driving became a chore. A place close by would suit her best.

Maggie rested her head on Faith's knee. Petting the dog, Faith looked at her. "I'll miss you, Maggie. But I don't think I can do it all. I'll find someone to take you. You'll have a happy life." Tears blurred again. She loved this dog. How could she give her away? Yet how could she care for her in the months to come if she needed another round of chemotherapy?

When they returned to the apartment, Faith called the doctor's office again, only to get the answering service because the office was closed for lunch. She left her name and number.

Returning to work, she tried to push aside the situation, focusing on the patients who came in, on the work she needed to do. But she couldn't shake the feeling of impending doom.

At four-thirty, she went to the front. The waiting room was empty. Marjorie was writing on the desk calendar.

"Did I get any calls?" Faith asked.

The older woman looked up. "A couple, but you were busy. And this is a place of business. I'm not your social secretary." She moved some papers and came up with two pink messages, handing them to Faith. The doctor had called twice.

"This is important. If he calls again, please come find me," Faith said, annoyed to have missed the calls, annoyed with Marjorie's attitude. But she was too worried to deal with the older woman now.

She hurried back to her phone and called, but, of course, the doctor was busy. She asked to speak to his nurse. Explaining the situation, the other nurse promised to look up what she could find and call her back.

Faith waited by the phone. The last of their patients had been seen. The cleaning of the exam rooms could wait. Ten minutes later when the phone rang, Faith went to the door to the waiting room.

"Yes, she's here. Hold, please." Marjorie looked at her. "Call for you."

Faith went to talk to the nurse. Five minutes later she hung up, not reassured at all. Dr. Stephens had not sent her file—that didn't mean anything either way. He obviously didn't think the situation was urgent enough to pass on while he was gone. He'd be back in two weeks. Fourteen endless days to wait to learn her fate.

Could it be something minor, like anemia?

If only Marjorie had given her the message last Friday, she could have had an answer before he left on vacation. Now it looked as if she had to wait another week. It wasn't fair!

There was also nothing Faith could do about it, except pray for patience. And hope.

On Wednesday Faith decided she couldn't go to the singles group. She called Janette to tell her not to expect her.

"Are you sick?" Janette asked, concerned.

"Maybe I'm coming down with something. Anyway, I'm staying home tonight."

"Okay. Let me know if you need anything."

Faith hung up, feeling sad about the prospect of moving back to Portland—if the diagnosis proved to be what she suspected. The not knowing was driving her crazy.

Shortly before nine-thirty that night the phone rang. It was Tate.

"You doing okay?" he asked.

"Fine."

"Janette said she thought you were sick."

"Maybe catching something," she said. "How was the meeting?"

"We finalized plans for bringing in the donations. Two guys have trucks we can use and I have the SUV. Some of the folks are coming down with their donations." He paused. "The Bible study was on Philippians."

"Sorry I missed it." Sorry she missed seeing him again. Time seemed so fleeting now. She clutched the phone, wishing she could see him, knowing she could not until she knew for certain what lay ahead. And if it was the worst, then she'd have to end her meetings with Tate entirely. She loved him too much to subject him to what he went through with Mandy.

The knowledge that she loved him hit her like a ton of bricks.

"I have to go," she said, stunned at the feelings that seeped through her. She loved Tate Johnson! How had that happened? She was going to guard her heart. Hadn't she learned anything from Allen? Not that she could put Tate in the same league as Allen. But he wasn't ready for a new relationship. And he deserved so much more than what she could offer.

"I'll check with you tomorrow," he said.

She wanted to tell him not to, but couldn't say the words. He was so kind and caring. If only things had been different.

Faith kept to herself Thursday and Friday. She went home for lunch, spent time with Maggie and the puppies and then returned to work. Friday on the way home, she picked up a Portland paper. She'd start looking for a place there—just in case.

Tate escorted another couple up the aisle of the church and to one of the spaces remaining in the crowded church. His duties as usher kept him busy, as more and more members of the church and community arrived for the celebration of the marriage of Gillian and Joe. He kept an eye out for Faith. When the signal came for the ushers to proceed up the aisle to stand at the groom's side, he scanned the crowded sanctuary one last time. Where was she? Had he missed her arrival?

He spotted Dr. Mallory so he knew there couldn't be an emergency at the clinic. It had closed early for the wedding. Where was Faith?

Joe came from the side door at the front and walked to the center, turning to look down the aisle. The wedding march began and Tate knew exactly when Joe saw Gillian by the way his face lit up and his eyes focused on the vision of loveliness coming toward him. Today the happy couple would begin their lives together. He prayed the Lord would bless them for many years to come.

Tate waited for the anguished memory of his own wedding, but instead, a peaceful nostalgia swept through him. Mandy had been lovely, just like Gillian was today. He missed her still, but the overwhelming pain of loss was missing. They'd had so much happiness. He'd cling to those memories and let the rest fade. She was gone. She wasn't coming back. *Goodbye, my love,* he said silently.

Swallowing a lump in his throat, Tate searched the rows of guests. He didn't see Faith. Had she not come after all? A moment later, he watched as Gillian became Joe's wife and reached out to take his hand, her eyes shining with love.

The ceremony didn't take long. When the newly married couple walked back down the aisle a few minutes later, Tate stepped up and escorted Marcie, who was one of the bridesmaids. He was amused at Zack escorting tiny Maud Stevens, Gillian's ninety-some-year-old matron of honor.

Once the sanctuary emptied, the wedding party returned for pictures. Tate drew on his patience as he longed to get to the reception hall to see if he'd just missed Faith, or if she truly had not attended.

Pictures over, he followed the bride and groom to the crowded reception. Quickly walking through, he looked for her everywhere. Then he headed outside to call her.

"Hello?" She answered just before it would have gone to voice mail.

"Faith, are you all right?" he asked. So she hadn't come. Why not?

"Oh, hi, Tate. Umm, I'm doing okay."

"You didn't come to the wedding."

"No. I, uh, just wasn't up to it."

"Honey, you can't let the past dictate the future."

"What? I just couldn't come today. Is the ceremony over?"

"The marriage vows were exchanged, now we're celebrating."

"Have fun."

"Want me to save you a piece of wedding cake?" he asked, not wanting to end the call.

"No. I've got to go. 'Bye."

Tate closed the phone and slipped it into his pocket. What was that about? Why the change of heart? Was she sick? She hadn't felt well earlier in the week. Maybe she was coming down with something. Not surprising. He often wondered why doctors and nurses weren't constantly ill, with all the sickness they were exposed to.

Returning to the reception, Tate went through the motions of enjoying himself. He would do nothing to dampen the festive mood for Joe and Gillian. But he couldn't completely enjoy himself because Faith hadn't come.

When the cake had been cut and the bridal couple seen off in a rain of birdseed, Tate considered his duties done. He took the plate of wedding cake he'd gotten for Faith and headed to her apartment. Climbing the stairs a few minutes later, he heard Maggie barking. A good watchdog, he thought. Not that there was a lot of crime in Rocky Point. But a single woman living alone couldn't be too careful.

He knocked on the door. A moment later Faith opened it. Tate was startled to see she'd been crying. The wedding had been too much of a reminder of love gone bad. His heart ached for her.

"I brought you some cake," he said, holding it out. "It's good luck to have wedding cake."

She stared at the plate, her eyes welling with tears. Slowly she reached out to take it. "Thank you," she said.

"You okay?"

She nodded.

She didn't look okay. How far dare he push? "I could come in for a while, tell you about the wedding."

Shaking her head, she glanced at him, then looked back at the piece of cake. "Not today. I have to go."

She closed the door in his face.

Tate drew in a breath. Maybe he shouldn't have brought the cake. If weddings reminded her of the man who had deserted her at the first sign of trouble, she'd be sad. Maybe it had hit her harder than she expected. But truly, she was better off without the guy.

She needed someone she could depend on. Someone who wouldn't bail when things started going awry.

Turning he walked down the stairs.

Someone like him?

He looked up at her apartment, wishing he had more of a right to barge in and demand to know what was wrong.

He opened the car door. Friends, he'd insisted.

Which meant he had to stifle his true impulses and find the strength to walk away.

Chapter Eight

Faith spent Saturday with Maggie and the puppies. It was a bittersweet time. She loved these dogs and laughed at the antics of the puppies who were growing more and more adventuresome each day. She sat beside Maggie on the floor and watched them indulgently. She imagined Maggie felt the same way. Cute as could be, but a bit wild.

She nibbled on the cake Tate had brought, praying for happiness and a long marriage for Joe and Gillian. She hardly gave Allen a thought. *Help me, Father, not be envious of what others have. I know You have a plan for me. If this is it, help me accept it with grace.*

Taking Maggie for a long walk just before dark helped her sleep that night. But in the morning she awoke to the feeling of impending doom. She debated attending church, but just couldn't face anyone. Instead, she took her Bible and let it fall open. Reading Paul's statement about the thorn in his side, she wondered if cancer was hers. She had thought Marjorie was. Paul wrote about persevering through hardships and prison. Could she do less? She would fight this invasive enemy with everything she had.

She'd cling to the hope the Lord had given her two years ago. Nothing diminished His love. And if life on earth was to end soon, she knew where she was heading. Peace was hard-won, but sustaining. She hugged the Bible to her heart as she prayed for peace, for contentment and for fortitude to face whatever the future held.

Janette called her after church.

"Hey, we missed you today. You must be under the weather."

"I'm doing okay." Sooner or later she'd have to tell her new friends. But she wanted to hold off until she'd talked to her physician. Once again, she hoped *anomalies* meant anemia or something else relatively benign. But for the oncologist to leave that message, it had to be serious. "Just not up to attending church."

"Pastor John gave an awesome talk about commitment and stepping out in faith. He does such good sermons, always referring to Bible verses I can look up and remember."

Stepping out in faith sounded like what she needed to cling to. "I'm sorry I missed it." Faith looked at Maggie, who was gazing at her with adoration. She liked her new church. If she licked the cancer again, she'd see about coming back to Rocky Point. But that was in the future. She had to get through the next few months first.

"Janette, do you know of anyone who might like a well-behaved dog?"

"You still trying to get rid of those puppies? I thought they were all spoken for."

"They are. And they should be ready to leave in a

couple more weeks. I was thinking of Maggie. She's only two—a wonderful dog." Her voice broke on the end. Blinking back tears, Faith drew a deep breath, trying to smile at her dog.

"I thought you were going to keep her," Janette said.

"I'm not sure I'll be able to for the long haul. Nothing definite, but if you hear of anyone, let me know, okay?"

"Sure. I'll ask around. If you want to take a trip or something, I'm sure someone in the singles group would watch her while you're gone."

"Thanks." That was an idea. Maybe she could prevail on someone and, if she made it, come back to claim Maggie. It was a better thought than giving her up altogether.

"And speaking of the group, it's two weeks to the rummage sale. We'll be finalizing plans this Wednesday. Sign up early for your shift—that way you get the best pick. Last year I dithered and ended up with closing on the second day. It gets frantic because we slash prices and everyone comes back to see what bargains they can get before closing time."

"I'll keep that in mind," Faith said, wondering where she'd even be when the rummage sale was held.

"Want to get together for lunch one day?" Janette asked.

"I'll see how things go and call you," Faith said, not willing to make plans.

Half an hour after their phone call ended, there was a knock on the door. When Faith answered, Tate stood there. Dressed casually, his dark hair was mussed, as if he'd run his fingers through it. The slight scar from his encounter with the boat a few weeks ago showed red. The grim look on his face spoke volumes.

"So I just got a call from Janette that something's wrong and we both want to know what it is," he said, stepping forward. "I'm here to find out."

Faith gave way and he entered the apartment.

He glanced around, noting the paper on the table, the puppies clamoring to greet him. He looked at her.

"I just wasn't up to going to church," she said. Sweeping her hand around, she encompassed the apartment. "Everything's fine here, as you can see."

"You didn't come to the wedding. To the singles group last week, to church this morning. Something's definitely wrong. Jenny was disappointed not to see you. She wanted to come see her puppy again." He sighed heavily. "And Zack and Marcie said Gillian noticed you hadn't attended yesterday. Janette said you're looking for a home for Maggie. Now that's definitely something. I thought you loved that dog."

Faith licked her lips and stared at him, uncertain how to respond. "I, umm, might have to move back to Portland. I won't be able to afford a place that has a yard and Maggie's happy here. If I do have to go, then I want to find her a good home, with someone who will love her."

"You love her. You keep her."

She looked away. "I will if I can. But if I can't, she needs a really good home."

Tate reached out his hand and took her chin, gently turning her to face him. "So what's up?" His fingers felt warm against her skin.

Faith wanted to reach out and let him enfold her in his arms, lend her some of his strength. She wanted to belong, to have someone there for her, so she didn't feel so alone. But looking into his dear face, she knew she couldn't do that. She couldn't pull him into the misery that might come. He'd been through so much with his wife. She'd never subject him to that again—not even as friends.

She shrugged, trying to maintain a casual air. "This and that. Who knows what the future will bring? I'm making contingency plans." She could hardly breathe with him so close, with the concern reflected in his dark eyes. His fingers hadn't moved. She never wanted to move, but she had to.

"I'm not leaving until you tell me what's going on," he said, his gaze steadfast, his fingers warm against her skin.

"Oh, Tate, you really don't want to know. Please, let's just say we're friends and as a friend, you'll leave me to find my own way." She reached up to hold his wrist, feeling the strength in his arm, hoping she had enough strength for the future. His pulse beat strong against her fingertips. She wished she could cling forever.

"I can't do that. Tell me. It must be serious." He frowned in thought for a moment, then narrowed his gaze.

"Allen's trying to get back together with you," he guessed.

Faith smiled sadly at that thought. "He would never do that," she said. And even if he did, she wouldn't make that mistake twice. "You're a good man, Tate. Thank you for your friendship."

How I wish it could have been undying love.

"You sound as if you're leaving," he said.

"I might be returning to Portland. Things are still up in the air right now."

"Why move to Portland? I thought you liked Rocky Point?"

"I do. It's just, maybe I don't know for sure." But she felt it was a sure thing. Every moment in his company was a memory she could take with her. She didn't want to leave. Yet she couldn't stay if the cancer had returned.

"What *do* you know for sure?" he asked, a hint of exasperation in his tone as he dropped his hand, breaking the connection she'd felt.

"That you need to go. I'm fine," she said raising her chin slightly. She felt even more alone when he stepped away.

"That's it. Go? Ignore what's bothering you? That's not going to happen, Faith. I said I wanted to know what's going on and I'm staying right here until you tell me." He sat down on the sofa. "Might as well tell me now as later," he said, leaning back, his long legs stretched out in front of him.

If he wasn't going to go until he knew, then she might as well tell him. How best to word it? How to let him know she expected nothing from him? He shouldn't be concerned. She would manage as she had before.

She stared at him, not knowing how to tell him. "I might have had a relapse," she blurted finally.

"A relapse to what?"

"Cancer."

He stared at her, the shock clearly evident. "I thought you said you were cancer-free."

"I thought I was. I had the surgery, chemo. I did everything I was supposed to. I prayed for healing. I found the Lord and thought that would be the beginning of a wonderful new life." She exhaled slowly. "I've enjoyed most of the past two years. But at my semiannual checkup there were anomalies."

"What does that mean?" he asked.

"I'm not sure," she admitted, averting her eyes. "I didn't get my physician's message when it first came in. By the time I found it, I was told the office is closed until next week because the doctor's on vacation." She crossed the room and sat on the edge of the sofa. Her legs wouldn't hold her anymore. "Now I won't find out if the cancer's returned until he gets back."

He shifted slightly to face her. "You don't look sick," he said.

"Yeah, well, I don't feel sick, either. But I didn't before, either. It was almost a fluke the cancer was discovered early, due to new blood testing that they offered to staff at the hospital." She sighed. "Ovarian cancer is often a silent killer because by the time there are any symptoms, the disease has progressed to the almost incurable stage."

"So they took bloodwork and there are anomalies. What else could it be?" Tate asked carefully.

"Anemia. Or some other blood disease, but that's unlikely. Diabetes maybe. I don't know. As I said, I have to wait another week to find out. But if the cancer has recurred, I'll need to go to Portland for treatment. We don't have that capability at the clinic."

He rose and paced across the room, turning to look at her. "You've been living with this for how long?"

"I found out on Tuesday."

"Why didn't you tell me?"

"Because I didn't want you to know."

Tate looked as if she'd slapped him. "Why not?"

"I don't want you to feel obligated in any way. I'm not your wife."

He studied her for a moment. "You're not my wife, but the way things were going, you could have been."

Faith felt a jolt. "What do you mean?"

He balled his hands into fists "I mean you and I have something special between us. I've never felt this way about another woman, since Mandy died. I have a dozen reasons why I shouldn't be falling in love, but they don't seem to matter."

"Please don't think you have to be the white knight, riding to the rescue. I don't know for sure that the cancer's back." And if it had recurred, the last person she would cling to would be Tate. He'd been through enough heartache.

"But you wouldn't be asking for someone to take your dog if you didn't think that."

She shrugged. "I'm just making contingency plans."

He studied her for a moment, then crossed back to the sofa, pulling her up into a tight embrace. "Marry me, Faith."

"No," she said, burying her face against his shoulder, breathing in the scent of him. She would never move from this spot if she could have one wish in life. Yet she couldn't stay. She soaked up the sensation of his strong arms holding her, of his heart beating against hers, of the might-have-beens if life were more fair.

"Why not?" he said, resting his cheek against her hair.

"Not as long as there's a possibility I'll be sick again. I would never do that to you," she said, her voice muffled.

Pushing away slightly, she did her best to smile up at him. "I'll be okay. I have a lot of friends in Portland. They stood by me last time. They'll rally again."

"Friends aren't family."

"No, but I've been without family for most of my life, Tate. I know how to handle that."

"I'll pester you until you give in," he said, gazing into her eyes.

She laughed at that. "No, you won't. My answer is no. Thank you, though. I'll always remember that you asked."

He studied her expression, obviously believing her. He gave her a sweet kiss then he left.

Faith waited until she heard his car drive off before bursting into tears. The greatest thing she could have wished for in Rocky Point would be to find a family, a man to love, a man to build a future with. Only it had come at the wrong time.

Why, Lord? Why Tate? How could I put him through the very thing that had been so hard for him with his wife? I couldn't. You know I couldn't. Please, let him know this is the right decision. Please, take care of him. I would have loved to have been his wife.

She sat on the sofa. Maggie came over and rested her head on Faith's knee.

"I know, girl. We're both sad. I hope I don't have to give you away, too." *Please, Father, please, be with me. Heal me if it's Your will. If not, give me the courage to face the next step in my journey.*

When the phone rang later, Faith almost didn't answer it. She was sure it was Tate and she wasn't up to battling with him.

It was Dr. Mallory. "Faith, Tate just filled me in. Why didn't you say something? Meet me at the clinic. We'll draw blood and take it to the lab today. There are emergency services for accident victims who need results right away." He cleared his throat. "We'll say this is an emergency. That way we'll find out about the anomalies long before your oncologist returns. I'll be there in ten."

"You don't have to do that," she protested. But hope flared. If they got the lab results back tomorrow, at least she'd *know.*

"I do. I can't have the best nurse I've ever had talking about returning to Portland. Ten minutes." He hung up before she could protest.

Faith gave thanks that Tate was the kind of man he was and went to get her shoes. She arrived at the clinic only moments after the doctor. Tate was there, chatting with Dr. Mallory.

"I could wait another week," she protested weakly when she joined them.

"No need. We'll find out what's up. I can't believe it's serious or Stephens wouldn't have left without making sure you knew. And started treatment right away."

"I had a message to call him before he left."

"Which you didn't get in time," Tate said.

Dr. Mallory raised an eyebrow. "Why not?"

Tate shrugged.

"I think Marjorie forgot to give it to me," Faith admitted. Deliberately forgot, but since that couldn't be proved, she'd keep those thoughts to herself.

"Come on through here. Too bad you can't do it yourself. I've heard patients comment on how well you give shots or take blood. They hardly feel a thing." The doctor led the way to one of the exam rooms.

She watched as several vials of blood were drawn. Then the doctor wrote out a handful of request slips, taping them to the different vials. He then put them into a carrying case and handed it to Tate.

Faith looked at him. "What are you doing?"

"I volunteered to take the blood to the lab. It's in Monkesville."

"Can you do that? It's Sunday."

"I don't know how busy they are. There's a reduced staff on weekends, but they're open seven days a week. I know Paul Murray, the director. I've already spoken with him. He'll expedite the blood tests," Dr. Mallory said. "With luck, we'll know something pretty quick. Better to know the full extent today or tomorrow than wait another week."

"Thank you," she said. She smiled at the doctor and then Tate. "Thanks for taking it over."

"I'm waiting for my yes," he said as he left.

"Yes to what?" the doctor asked when the sheriff left.

"He asked me to marry him. But I can't. Not unless I'm healthy and likely to remain so. Even then, I'm not sure it's fair to him if I say yes. I think he's just being kind, wanting to give me support at a time of need." She swallowed hard. "You see…I can't have kids. Tate's so good around children, he should have a bunch of his own. I know his parents want grandchildren."

"The man knows what he wants. Funny, I've known him most of his life and I never thought he was especially kind—not enough to put his own life in disarray just to be kind to someone else. And I've heard the rumors running around. You're the first woman he's shown any interest in since he moved back to town," the doctor said as he cleaned up. Then he looked at her. "And he'd be lucky if you did say yes."

Faith flushed with pleasure at the doctor's words. "Thank you. Still, I need to know where I stand before

I make any decision along those lines." And she'd have to make sure Tate was all right with not having children. Allen hadn't been. She couldn't bear it if, down the line, Tate resented her inability to have a baby.

"With luck, we'll know something soon. Next time something like this comes up, tell me. No need to carry the burden alone," the doctor chided.

"I'm not alone, I have the Lord on my side," she said, conscious that she had more than that with the help of her boss and the sheriff.

"Ecclesiastes says, two are better than one—if either of them falls down, one can help the other up. But pity anyone who falls and has no one to help them up." He raised a brow. "That's not you, Faith. You've made a lot of friends in town. We'll all be there for you to help you face this. Don't forget that."

"I won't. Thank you, doctor."

"And we'll have a talk with Marjorie in the morning," he said as they were leaving.

Tate drove swiftly to the lab in Monkesville. He was still stunned that Faith had received bad news—and that she'd kept it to herself for so long. Didn't she understand that her friends would want to help, if only to support her with prayers? Maybe not. She'd said she was a new Christian. Maybe she didn't fully understand the power of prayer or the support other Christians could offer.

Please, Father, if it be Your will, let her be all right. Let the anomalies be minor, quickly healed. Let her live a long and faithful life serving You and being a witness to others. And help me, Father. I think I love her. No, I know I love her. The question is, am I strong enough to endure whatever might come? I don't think

I can face another life wasting away. Tate wished he was different, that he'd plunge in wherever he was needed. But could he do that a second time?

Yet Faith had no one. Mandy had had her parents, her brother, Tate and Tate's family, plus numerous friends and other relatives. Faith was alone, except for a foster family who barely kept in touch and friends. But friends weren't the same as family.

"If she married me, she'd have all the family she'd need," he said aloud. He'd asked her spontaneously. Now that he had time to think about it, the full ramifications of what marriage to her could entail struck him with full force. Life didn't come with guarantees. He had his faith and trust in the Lord. And his love for Faith. Could he do this again?

Unceasing faith. The words echoed in his mind. *I put my trust in You, Lord.*

The lab was on the far side of Monkesville. It was practically deserted by the time Tate got there. In a flash, the technicians had logged in the blood, promising to get the results to the doctor first thing in the morning. Tate had no choice but to leave it at that, much as he wanted to urge them to run their tests immediately.

He used the drive home to pray, think of what could be done if the cancer had recurred. Praying again for healing. First thing he'd do was call Pastor John and start the prayer chain. It hadn't been too long ago this summer that Marcie's dad had been on the prayer chain. He was recovering from a kidney transplant and doing even better than the doctors expected. Tate knew better than to underestimate the power of prayer.

Yet, he'd prayed long and hard, as had others, for Mandy. No one knew the Father's plan. That didn't mean he couldn't trust the Lord to know best. And hope for a complete recovery and a long and happy life for Faith. With him.

When Tate reached town, he stopped at his house to call Pastor John. He asked if the pastor had some free time and was immediately invited to come to the pastor's home. Tate called the doctor to update him, then took off to visit Trinity's pastor.

"Hi, Tate. Come on out back. We'll be alone there. Virginia and the kids are preparing dinner and there's always a lot of commotion with that task," Pastor John greeted him when he arrived.

They walked to the shade in the backyard and sat on chairs on the patio. "What can I do for you?" the pastor asked.

"First, I need for the prayer chain to get going praying for Faith. She's kept it quiet, but I don't think she'd mind my talking about this…" He took a deep breath before continuing. "She had ovarian cancer a couple of years ago. She went through surgery and chemo and thought she had it licked, but this week she received bad news. We don't know the full extent yet, but it could be a recurrence of the disease. I'd like prayer for healing."

"We can get right on that. But you could have called me to start the prayer chain," Pastor John said, looking at him with kind eyes. "What else?"

Tate nodded. "I wanted to talk to you about me. Me and Faith."

"Faith as in belief in God, or the young nurse we'll begin praying for?"

"Both, actually." Tate realized that's where his main problem came from. His lack of strong faith to trust in God to do best for all. How did a man regain his faith when it had been damaged?

Funny how everything seemed to have changed, Faith thought as she walked with Maggie along the marina. Just a few weeks ago, Tate had plunged into the water to rescue that child. She had never met him before. Now she was in love with him, yet couldn't do anything about it. Even if this scare proved manageable, there would be others. She might make her five years and be considered cured, but the specter of cancer would forever hang over her.

And the children she had once hoped to have—that would never come to be. For some reason the Lord saw fit to have her live without any blood relatives. She had some wonderful friends, whom she loved and who loved her in return. She needed to remember that. Cherish what she had and not yearn for what she could not have. Hadn't she just read in the Bible this weekend when Paul said he'd learned to be content, whatever his circumstances? She needed to follow that example and be content with what she had. For however long she had it.

It was a wonderful time to be alive. Modern medicine was available to fight the insidious disease. Friends had rallied around her before. They'd do it again. And now she had even more friends.

And she had Maggie. For as long as she could keep her. And even if she had to give her up, she'd remember these weeks. If the Lord let her be cured, she'd see about getting another dog.

When she returned home, Faith was surprised to

see Tate sitting on the bottom step, a big white paper bag beside him, Marcie's café's logo emblazoned on it.

"I brought dinner," he said. "I know it's sort of late, but you haven't eaten, have you?"

"No, I haven't. Thank you. You didn't have to do that," she said, holding the leash to prevent Maggie from grabbing their dinner and scarfing it down. What a special thing to do.

Tate lifted the bag and stood up. "This is for me and your mistress, Maggie girl. You have a yummy doggie dinner upstairs."

"Yuck, how they like that stuff's beyond me. But it's nutritious and the way she wolfs down the food, she must like it," Faith said, happy to see him. She wanted to be strong, send him away and carry on by herself. But as Doc Mallory had wisely said, two were better than one. As long as she kept their relationship at the friendship level. Which was hard when she just wanted him to hug her and promise that things would turn out okay.

The shrimp sandwiches and coleslaw were delicious. Faith had more of an appetite today than she'd had all week. Due, she knew, to the help she'd received once Tate and the doctor had found out her concerns.

"So the lab said results will be available tomorrow. They'll call the doctor first thing."

"I hope he gets the call," she murmured. Maybe she should arrange to be in the reception area until the call came through.

"What's going on with Marjorie?" Tate asked.

She wiped her mouth with a napkin. "What makes you think anything is going on?" she asked.

"A couple of things you've said. So?"

"She wanted her niece to get the job. I think she believes if work becomes uncomfortable enough for me, I'll leave. She's always saying how many more opportunities there are in Portland."

Tate nodded. "True. But what you don't know is that the doctor interviewed her niece two weeks before interviewing you. If he'd wanted her, he would have hired her and not kept the position open for so long."

Faith stared at him. "Truly?"

He nodded. "She's fresh out of nursing school. Doesn't have nearly the experience you have. In a small-town clinic like this, medical workers have to be able to pitch in with a lot of different skills. Your time in the E.R. obviously paid off. Heather still has years of work to catch up to you." He shrugged. "So if you left tomorrow, Heather still wouldn't get that job. Someone should remind Marjorie about that. And you should have told the doctor you were having problems."

"She's been there for years. I kept hoping things would get better. I didn't want to cause trouble," she admitted. "I like my job, love the town. I wanted to work harmoniously with her."

"Work relationships are not one-sided. She has to meet you halfway. And if she can't, then changes might need to be made," Tate said firmly.

Faith nodded. "Though the changes could be me returning to Portland for treatment," she said wistfully.

When they finished, Faith quickly cleaned up, stumbling over puppies who were always underfoot these days. She laughed. "I'll miss these guys when they go to their new homes."

"Jenny can't wait. I suspect the others feel the same way. Kids and puppies—that's one thing that makes families. Our family had dogs when my sister and I were growing up." He looked sad for a moment. "I still miss the last one. But once I left for college, my folks weren't as excited about keeping dogs. So after he died, they didn't get another one. Dogs do require daily care."

"Kids and puppies," she repeated, staring at the dogs. "Foster parents do a lot, you know, taking in kids, raising them to the best of their abilities. I guess the added burden of pets is something they can't handle. I wish I'd had a puppy when I was younger."

He grinned. "Well, you've certainly made up for it with this brood."

"I have, haven't I? What fun I've had!" She needed to focus on that. She'd had a blast living in Rocky Point. If this stage of her life ended, she had wonderful memories.

"And lots more to come," Tate said.

She shrugged. "I'm trying to adopt Paul's stance—be content with whatever I have."

"I think you should adopt the Lord's stance—life more abundant."

"It's been abundant here," she said with a smile, wiping the last of the counter and rinsing out the dishrag. She'd miss it so if she had to leave.

Tate came to the counter and reached for her hands, still wet.

"Faith, I love you. I didn't expect to fall in love again. I loved Mandy. But she's gone and I did fall in love again." His voice grew hoarse with emotion. "I can't imagine my life without you. I want to hear your laughter in the morning, see you across the dining table each night. I want to show you all that life in a small town can offer. Show you what I can offer. Please, would you marry me?"

She shook her head. "No, Tate. You don't know what might happen. If the cancer has returned, it could mean the end. At the very least another round of chemo, which is so enervating. I can't deal with emotional entanglements and keep focused on getting well. Thank you. I wish my answer could be different, but I have to say no, again."

"I had a talk with Pastor John before I came over. Everything's a muddle. But I know one thing—I believe. I believe in the Lord. I believe that the Creator of the universe has everything under His control." He squeezed her hands and gazed deep into her eyes. "No one said this life's journey would be easy. But the things that keep it going are love and family and faith in the Lord. I want you as my wife, for me to love and cherish and walk beside for as long as we have. I think you care for me, right?"

Faith couldn't lie. She nodded. Pulling her hands free, she quickly dried them on a towel. "I love you, Tate, and that's why I can't marry you. It wouldn't be fair."

"Hey, life's not fair. But it can be glorious. We'll face this together and, Lord willing, we'll come through on the other side."

She yearned to accept the love he offered. "It's not fair to you," she repeated, hoping she could remain firm in her decision. The temptation to give in, to let him share the burden, was strong. But her resolve was stronger.

"It's fair if I say so." He reached out and pulled her closer. "Marry me, Faith. I thought I couldn't deal with something like this again. But the pastor helped me see that my faith in the Lord is the one true thing in life that will never change. I might stumble and even fall, but the Lord's there to pick me up and set me on my feet again. Let me be there to help you get on your feet again. I love you, Faith."

"I love you, Tate," she said, giving that much.

He kissed her gently, then more passionately. Lifting his head he grinned down at her.

"I'm waiting for the yes," he prompted.

"After—"

"No, now! We'll confront the future together!"

Dare she risk it. Could she have enough faith in what he said?

"What if—"

"We step out in unceasing faith," he said, his gaze holding hers.

"If you're sure—"

He gave a shout and picked her up, twirling them around to the accompaniment of Maggie's barking and the puppies yipping. Laughing, he leaned his head back and shouted, "She said yes, Lord. Thank You!"

Faith laughed at his delight. "I haven't yet, but I will. Yes!"

He kissed her again, then set her back down. "I wish you had a rooftop deck so I could go up and shout it from there. We could go out on the top of the steps."

She giggled. "Silly. It's enough to know you want me no matter what."

"If I were sick, what would you do?" he asked, tenderly pushing back some of her blond curls.

"Care for you the best I could." There was no doubt about that. She'd do anything for him.

"Me, too. Come on, let's go tell my parents."

"Oh." Faith's smile faded. "Your mom's going to be so disappointed. I heard her talk about wishing for grandkids. She doesn't know, does she, that I can't have children?"

"Marriage isn't only about children, Faith. It's about two people pledging their lives together, and making their way—together. If we decide we want kids, we'll adopt. There are lots of kids left alone, just as you were, who need loving parents."

"They won't be yours," she said sadly.

"Of course they would be—yours, too." He ducked his head to see her better. "Do you love Maggie?"

"Yes. She's a sweetheart."

"She's a dog, actually. But how long did it take you to fall for her?"

"About ten minutes."

"And you think you couldn't love babies just because someone else gave birth to them?" he asked.

"I would love a baby, a small child. I like kids." Hope began to blossom. He really wouldn't mind adopting?

"Me, too. So after a few years of having you to myself, maybe we'll adopt. We'll see how it goes. We'll see what the Lord has in mind."

Faith nodded. They'd have to be sure she was going to make it for the long haul. She just hoped his parents would feel the same way.

The next morning, Faith was on top of the world. Both Todd and Cecile Johnson had been thrilled with the news and welcomed her so sweetly into their family. She hadn't gotten to bed until after midnight as they discussed wedding plans and other contingencies. She and Tate had explained the medical issues and the possible ramifications. Distressed at the news, they offered support and help however they could. Once,

Faith caught Cecile looking at Tate as if to judge how he would handle things. Whatever she saw reassured her, because she nodded and looked back at Faith with a warm smile.

To her surprise, neither of Tate's parents seemed concerned about her inability to have children.

"I was adopted and adored my parents," Cecile said. "We would welcome whatever baby you two have into our family. How could we not love another child?"

Faith had been torn between tears and laughter most of the evening. She had never expected such an instant embrace, as they enveloped her as part of their family. Her family, as soon as she and Tate married—both the Johnsons had insisted on that.

Dr. Mallory was already at the clinic when she arrived.

"Have you heard anything?" she asked. Fear warred with hope. She took a breath, trying to calm herself, but she anticipated the worst.

"Not yet."

Marjorie came in and looked at them both. "Good morning," she said. She frowned. "Is something going on?"

"Good morning. I'm expecting an important call from Hunter Labs. Please find me wherever I am when it come is. I can't miss that call," the doctor said.

"Sure. I'll make sure you get it," Marjorie said, glancing at Faith, then back to the doctor.

"I need to talk with you later, Marjorie, but I see Mrs. Denton is here for her appointment," the doctor said, turning to smile at their first patient as she entered the reception area.

Faith went back to get the file and greeted their patient when she came to the exam room. The routine of the day would keep her occupied until the lab called with results. She had prayed last night and again this morning for the anomaly to be easily handled. With Tate's love and support, she could face anything. But for his sake, she hoped it wasn't the cancer returning.

The call came in just before nine-thirty. Marjorie went to find the doctor, who, in turn, called Faith to join him in his office. "This concerns you, might as well be here."

She closed the door and watched as he picked up the phone. "Thanks for getting back to me so quickly," he said. He nodded his head several times, gave a couple of "hmms," and glanced at Faith once. "Could you fax the report over and then mail a hard copy? I want to make sure I have all that. Okay. Thanks again."

He hung up and looked at her.

"No anomalies," he said.

"What?" She hadn't expected that. "But, the earlier test. The one Dr. Stephens did…" She sat down on one of the chairs. She didn't understand. "I'm really okay?"

"You're really okay. I don't know what Stephens thought was wrong, unless it was a false positive. They did every test I asked and came up with everything within the normal range. You are not even anemic. The results are from a healthy young woman in the prime of life."

Faith closed her eyes against tears and lifted up a prayer of thanks to the Lord. Her heart felt as if it would explode with happiness. She quickly opened her eyes. "I have to tell Tate. He insisted that I marry him, even before he knew I'd be okay."

"Run along. I want to have a talk with Marjorie."

Faith nodded, and jumped up, happiness threatening to overwhelm her. She couldn't call—she had to see Tate. Tell him the Lord had blessed her again and she was not sick. She scarcely gave a thought to the message she'd seen. A week of heartache and anguish vanished like the wind. She was healthy!

She ran all the way to city hall.

Two minutes later she burst into the sheriff's office.

The deputy looked up. "Good morning, Faith. Can I help you?"

"Is Tate in?"

"He is." Before the man could say anything further she raced down the hall, stopping at the door and looking at Tate. His head was bowed, his eyes closed. Was he praying?

"Tate."

He snapped up at that, took one look at her and dashed around the desk. "You're okay?" he asked.

She nodded, laughing, crying, reaching out to grab hold of him. "I'm fine. I'm not sick! Everything's in the normal range. Everything!"

He picked her up and twirled her around, setting her down on her feet and holding her so tightly she could scarcely breathe.

"Thank You, Lord," he whispered, kissing her, hugging her, thanking the Lord over and over. Faith echoed his heartfelt prayers. She was well, in love and going to marry the world's most wonderful man.

"Thank You, Lord," she said.

Chapter Nine

Tate drove her to the clinic and went in to speak to the doctor. There was no one in the reception area, but a sign on the counter said to have a seat and someone would be right with them.

"Dr. Mallory said he was going to talk to Marjorie," Faith said, glad there were no patients waiting.

"Then we'll wait a minute or two," Tate said, reaching out to hold her hand. "Once you're done with work, let's go to dinner. Here in town or Monkesville or even Portland, if you like."

"I'd love to have another dinner at your place, on your deck. According to locals, this nice warm weather won't last forever."

"I'll pick you up around six," he said, leaning in to give her a kiss just as Mrs. Baldwin walked in.

"Well, am I hearing wedding bells?" she teased, when the two sprang apart.

"You are, Mrs. Baldwin. You're the first to know that Faith has agreed to marry me."

"Oh, no, don't tell me that. You go home and tell your mama first thing. She'll skin you alive if she knows you're spreading the news around. She should know first," the older woman admonished. "I shan't tell a soul until I hear it from Cecile. Go on now. Don't let anyone else catch you canoodling."

Faith laughed. "Canoodling?"

"Maybe it's an old Rocky Point saying," Tate said with a shrug and a grin. "She's right—I'd be in big trouble if my folks didn't already know. We told them last night," he said to Mrs. Baldwin. "There are wedding plans to make." He gave a groan. "Good grief, am I going to hear about this from Zack and Joe. Especially Joe, after I was less than enthusiastic about sitting through endless hours discussing his wedding."

She laughed again. Faith could have danced around the reception area she was so happy.

"We could elope," she suggested. She didn't care about the wedding…she was looking forward to the marriage. To spend her life with Tate—how blessed could one woman be?

"Oh, no," Mrs. Baldwin said. "Nothing this town likes better than a wedding."

"And you deserve the best one we can afford— white dress, flowers and a huge reception at Trinity," Tate said.

"You already had a big wedding," she said.

"And I want another one—with you. The last one I'll ever have."

She smiled at him.

The door behind her opened and Marjorie came out looking subdued. She glanced at the two of them, started to say something and then saw Mrs. Baldwin.

"You were right, Marjorie," the older woman beamed. "Our Faith *was* interested in the sheriff. They're getting married!"

Marjorie looked at them, frowning slightly. "I wish you well," she said stiffly. She cleared her throat. "I need to speak with Faith—alone."

"See you at six," Tate said, tapping her chin with his finger.

Faith would have preferred another kiss, but conscious of the others in the room, appreciated Tate's more casual goodbye. There would be plenty of times in the years ahead for kisses—privately in their own home.

She was dazed at the thought of getting married, sharing her life with Tate forever.

"At six," she repeated and watched until he left.

Mrs. Baldwin sat in one of the chairs. "Hurry up, Marjorie."

Marjorie stepped back into the hall. Faith followed.

"I apologize for everything. I was unaware of the full situation. I thought if you left, my niece—never mind. I won't be doing anything like that again. And I should have given you your doctor's message immediately so you could have contacted him before he left for vacation. Again, I apologize, I had no idea how important it was." She took a deep breath. "I got it wrong, anyway. He said no anomalies." She didn't meet Faith's eyes, but kept hers on the wall behind her.

"That's all right. Actually, maybe it's better it all happened as it did." Faith wouldn't elaborate, but she'd never forget that Tate insisted she marry him before he knew she was well. She'd cherish that knowledge all her days.

Marjorie met her gaze then. "How better?"

"It showed Tate and me that his love was strong enough to deal with any challenge we might face together. He was worried he couldn't go through something like what happened with his first wife. I'll forever remember that even thinking my cancer had returned, he stood beside me. I might always have wondered."

Marjorie nodded. "I haven't been the easiest person to work with. I really thought my niece, Heather, would be the best one for the job. But Dr. Mallory told me just now that if he had not hired you, he still wouldn't have hired Heather. She lacks the experience he wants for our clinic. I will do better in the future."

Impulsively, Faith gave her a quick hug. "That's all we can ask for, is to try to do better as we go through life. We'll let bygones be bygones and start fresh."

Marjorie looked startled when Faith pulled back. "That's nice of you." She studied Faith's radiant expression. "You love Tate Johnson, don't you?"

"So much, you'll never know," Faith said with a big smile. She hoped the entire world realized that.

"He's a good man. Cecile and Todd have two fine children. I hope you two will be happy together. He'll be more likely to stay on as our sheriff if he has family and settles down in Rocky Point." She checked her watch. "Well, I'd better get back to work. Flo Bradshaw doesn't like to be kept waiting."

Faith received a half-dozen calls that afternoon, wishing her and Tate a wonderful life, asking about the wedding, saying how happy people were to hear the news. Faith missed most of them, but Marjorie made it a point to bring each message to Faith's station almost before the ink was dry.

When Janette called, Faith was between patients and took her call.

"Woohoo, friend. I'm so happy for you. But this

means you and Tate have to drop out of the singles group, and I'll miss you."

"We haven't even talked about the wedding, so we'll still be singles for a while longer—enough to help at the rummage sale," Faith said.

She had mixed emotions. She knew she'd always be fond of the people in the singles group who had made her feel so welcome. They'd see each other at church and around town. But Janette was right. She was no longer eligible. She was now officially part of a couple. She had a man to marry, a life to build together. And, if the Lord willed it, one or two children to adopt, make their own and raise with love and faith.

"I get to help with the wedding. I'm calling Cecile right now. You'll have your whole Trinity family to help out. It's going to be so much fun!" Janette said with glee.

Hanging up, Faith gave a brief prayer of thanksgiving for the happiness that almost overwhelmed her.

Just before the clinic closed for the day, Tate returned.

"I couldn't keep away," he said, walking into the back after Marjorie had told him they had no patients.

"Did you tell your parents the news?" she asked, tidying up her station. She kept looking at him with a smile. She loved him so, and now she knew he loved her.

"They are thrilled. They would have been with you every step of the way if the cancer had returned, but they're rejoicing now that it didn't. They asked us to go there for dinner—is that all right with you?"

"Sure. I've had a bunch of calls." She waved the pink message slips. "And I spoke with Janette. Everyone seems happy about this. But none can compare to how I feel."

"Or me." He drew her into his arms and kissed her. "Marry me really soon. I don't think I can wait long."

"I've been thinking about that all afternoon. And how Flo Baldwin said the town loves a wedding. Marcie and Zack are planning a Christmas wedding. How about we do ours in the spring? Maybe April? I think I'd like that."

"Then April it is, though that seems so far off."

"The time will fly by. And I want to enjoy being engaged, planning a wedding, inviting all our friends." She gazed up at him. "Let's enjoy the journey. Only yesterday, I never thought I'd find this kind of happiness. I want to savor every moment with you. I love you, Tate."

"And I love you, Faith, and always will."

He smiled at her and, having the right at long last, Faith reached out to touch that adorable dimple.

* * * * *

Dear Reader,

Welcome back to Rocky Point, Maine. Summer is winding down and soon the tourists will be going home. A new resident takes center stage when Faith Stewart moves to town. She soon meets Tate Johnson, Rocky Point's sheriff. As they end up spending more and more time together, they agree to just be friends. They both have baggage from the past holding them back from the future. But sometimes the best laid plans don't come about. What happens when friends fall in love? And then what happens when that love is tested?

I hope you'll enjoy the journey Faith makes in her new home. And in reconnecting with the people of Rocky Point. Above all I hope you see how her own faith strengthens her when she's faced with difficult decisions and an uncertain future.

Best,

Barbara McMahon

Questions for Discussion

1. When the story opens, Faith is newly arrived in Rocky Point. She's found the ideal job, but faces constant veiled animosity from a fellow employee. Have you had a similar situation? How did you handle it? Was Faith's manner one you would have chosen? Why or why not?

2. Joe Kincaid takes Tate home after his accident and talks excitedly about his upcoming wedding. In contrast, Tate remembers his own with aching loss. Do you think he truly wished his friend joy in his marriage? Could there be a touch of envy?

3. Faith found the dog and puppies in the rain and immediately took them into her home. Would you have done that or called Animal Control to pick them up? If you took them in, would you keep them until you found their owner, or only until authorities could pick them up? Do you think Faith began bonding with her new dog from that moment on?

4. Tate admires Faith for starting over in a new town where she knew no one. Have you ever had to do that? How did it go? Did you join a church to meet people as well as to worship? What other things did you do to make yourself feel more at home?

5. Faith joins a singles group and immediately plunges into the rummage-sale project. Do you feel this was the best way to get involved? Was

it strengthening her faith? How would you have handled this opportunity?

6. Tate is growing more and more interested in Faith, yet still has lingering feelings for his deceased wife. Do you think a person can move forward yet still hold love from the past? Why or why not?

7. When Marjorie's actions are discovered and she is reprimanded by the doctor, Faith is quick to forgive. Does this seem logical? How would you have handled the situation?

8. Tate went through a lot during his late wife's illness. Do you think he would shy away from becoming involved with another woman who had also fought a life-threatening illness? Does it ring true that love and faith could overcome a man's reluctance to take a chance on love again? How would you feel if the situation came to you?

9. Tate sees his love as strong and steadfast—no matter what the future holds. Does this seem in character, or would he be more likely to wait for the outcome before making a commitment? Have you known people in a similar situation? How did they handle things?

10. Faith plans to leave Rocky Point and return to Portland if her illness returns. Do you think this is a wise choice, or could she have handled it differently? What could have made a difference to her thinking?

11. Faith keeps quiet about her past, not wanting to get the same reaction as her longtime friends. Do you let an illness or situation define a person? Can you get past that to see who your friend really is, and give her space to decide if she wants to bring up the past or move on?

12. Do you think being a orphan, as Faith is, makes it that much harder to get through life, or, because she had to depend on herself so much, did that make her a stronger person? How would you have handled things?

INSPIRATIONAL

Wholesome romances that touch the heart and soul.

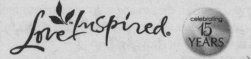

COMING NEXT MONTH
AVAILABLE FEBRUARY 28, 2012

LILAC WEDDING IN DRY CREEK
Return to Dry Creek
Janet Tronstad

DADDY LESSONS
Home to Hartley Creek
Carolyne Aarsen

TRIPLETS FIND A MOM
Annie Jones

A MAN TO TRUST
Carrie Turansky

HIGH COUNTRY HEARTS
Glynna Kaye

PICTURE PERFECT FAMILY
Renee Andrews